STARTING GUN

With the aid of a helpful lady of the night, Canyon O'Grady found his man in a crowded New Orleans saloon. The man who had committed ruthless murder in the shadow of the New Orleans cathedral. He was easy to spot—ugly as sin and twice as vicious.

"What do you want?" the man asked.

O'Grady took out his gun and pressed the barrel beneath the man's chin. "Either move or find your brains on the ceiling."

The man obeyed—too well. In a flash, he was out the door. When O'Grady followed, a gunshot greeted him.

The great Louisiana gold race was on—and the one who could outrun a bullet would win. . . .

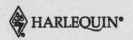

Coming Next Month

#3895 HER OUTBACK PROTECTOR Margaret Way
Men of the Outback

Sandra Kingston looks too young to be able to run the Moondai cattle station. Overseer Daniel Carson knows she will most likely need all the support he can give her. In the past Sandra has always been forced to fight her own battles, yet she can't deny that having Daniel close by her side makes her feel both protected...and desired.

#3896 THE DOCTOR'S PROPOSAL Marion Lennox
Castle at Dolphin Bay

Tragedy has left Dr. Kirsty McMahon afraid to fall in love, so when she meets commitment-phobic, gorgeous single father Dr. Jake Cameron, she assures herself that the chemistry between them will never amount to anything. But soon the attraction between them becomes too strong to ignore. Will they reconsider the rules they've made for themselves?

#3897 A WOMAN WORTH LOVING Jackie Braun
The Conlans of Trillium Island

Audra Conlan has always been fun, flamboyant and wild, until fate gives her a second chance. She will repent her mistakes, face her estranged family and evade men like photographer Seth Ridley, who's irresistible. But when her past threatens her new life, will Audra forgive the woman she once was, and embrace the woman she's meant to be...?

#3898 BLUE MOON BRIDE Renee Roszel

Roth Jerric may be drop-dead gorgeous, but he's Hannah Hudson's ex-boss, and the last person she wants around. Now they are no longer working together, and Roth can't understand why they're clashing more than usual—the tension is at breaking point. He's not looking for any romantic entanglement, but—try as he might—Hannah is one woman he can't ignore.

CANYON O'GRADY

23

LOUISIANA GOLD RACE

by

Jon Sharpe

SIGNET
Published by the Penguin Group
Penguin Books USA Inc., 375 Hudson Street,
New York, New York 10014, U.S.A.
Penguin Books Ltd, 27 Wrights Lane,
London W8 5TZ, England
Penguin Books Australia Ltd, Ringwood,
Victoria, Australia
Penguin Books Canada Ltd, 10 Alcorn Avenue,
Toronto, Ontario, Canada M4V 3B2
Penguin Books (N.Z.) Ltd, 182–190 Wairau Road,
Auckland 10, New Zealand

Penguin Books Ltd, Registered Offices:
Harmondsworth, Middlesex, England

First Published by Signet, an imprint of New American Library,
a division of Penguin Books USA Inc.

First Printing, January, 1993
10 9 8 7 6 5 4 3 2

Canyon O'Grady

His was a heritage of blackguards and poets, fighters and lovers, men who could draw a pistol and bed a lass with the same ease.

Freedom was a cry seared into Canyon O'Grady, justice a banner of his heart.

With the great wave of those who fled to America, the new land of hope and heartbreak, solace and savagery, he came to ride the untamed wildness of the Old West.

With a smile or a six-gun, Canyon O'Grady became a name feared by some and welcomed by others, but rememberd by all . . .

*Old New Orleans, where rumors of
hidden gold fueled greed that
tore men's souls in their mad
dash for wealth and power. . . .*

1

At night New Orleans shined, reflecting the light of the full moon that hung in the sky like a great pearl. Canyon O'Grady looked at the moon from his hotel window, listening to the deep, even breathing of the woman in the bed behind him. He turned to look at her. The moonlight coming through the window made her skin glow almost golden—like the gold O'Grady had been told was buried somewhere in the area.

O'Grady didn't know about the gold firsthand. Hell, he didn't even know about it secondhand. He had been informed by his superior, Major General Rufus Wheeler, and even *Wheeler* didn't get the information secondhand . . .

"Since when are we acting on second- and third-hand information?" O'Grady had asked.

He was seated in front of Wheeler's desk. The general sat behind his desk, lighting a cigar. He waited until he had it going to his satisfaction before shaking the match out and looking across the desk at O'Grady.

"We're talking about a lot of gold here, O'Grady," Wheeler said. "Gold that some people still think will finance a war between the South and the North."

"If fanatics buried this gold in anticipation of a

9

war," O'Grady said, "what makes you—us—think it's still there? Maybe it was already dug up. Maybe some of those fanatics have already split it up, and are living the high life in Mexico, or even Europe."

"No," Wheeler said, "the gold is still there. Gold doesn't mean the same thing to a fanatic that it means to a normal man, O'Grady. To him, it's a tool, like a gun. Its only value is in what it can do for his cause. Believe me, the gold is there, but it might not be for very much longer. The president is concerned that this war is much closer than anyone thinks. All the South needs is financing. This buried gold could put them over the top."

"If it exists," O'Grady said.

"If it exists," Wheeler said, "it's there, and you're going to find it before anyone else has a chance to."

"Does this information come from a reliable source?" O'Grady asked.

"No," Wheeler said frankly, "it doesn't, but we're taking the chance that it's accurate. After all, what have we got to lose?"

"Me?" O'Grady asked.

Of course, Canyon was no stranger to risking his life for his government, his *president,* his country. After all, if he wasn't doing that, what would he be doing?

The word was there was gold buried somewhere in Louisiana, most likely near New Orleans, *more* likely than not somewhere out in the bayou. According to their information—their thirdhand information, at best—there were others also looking for it. Canyon O'Grady realized that he was on a virtual gold hunt, and this was his starting point.

The woman on the bed stirred, and he turned and watched her stretch . . .

They had seen each other down in the casino, their eyes meeting across the room. He was playing poker, and she was playing blackjack. At that moment neither of them had wanted to abandon their streaks of good luck. Hers was the first to run out, and she drifted away from the table toward the restaurant. His cards finally started to go cold, and he also abandoned the tables for the dining room.

When he entered he saw that all of the tables were taken. The woman was sitting alone at one of them, and he approached her.

"May I sit?" he asked. "There don't seem to be any available tables."

"I don't mind sharing," she said.

He sat across from her and examined her close up, where previously he had only seen her from across the room.

She had hair the color of a raven's wing, and it was piled high atop her head, leaving her alabaster shoulders and long, graceful neck in view. She was wearing a dress that was cut low, revealing lots of creamy cleavage. She was a full-bodied woman without any hint of fat, tall and graceful even though grace usually seemed to belong to willowy women. He'd watched her walk away from the blackjack table, as had most of the men in the room, and she moved as if gliding, her feet a few inches off the floor.

"What do you think?" she asked.

"What is there to think?" he asked. "I have no choice but to find you beautiful and charming. To find you otherwise would make me either blind, or a fool, or worse, a liar."

"And you are none of those three?"

"I hope not."

"No," she said, cocking her head sideways to examine him in turn, "you are not."

"How can you tell?"

"Well, you're obviously not blind," she said, "and if you were a fool you would have left the table when we first noticed each other, even though you were winning. As for being a liar, you have much too honest a face for that."

"My name is Canyon O'Grady," he said.

"Lisa Carlson."

"Have you dined?"

"Not yet," she said. "I was waiting for you."

O'Grady raised his hand and a waiter hurried to their table.

"What would you like?" Canyon asked.

"Why don't you order for the both of us," she said. "It will be quicker that way, won't it?"

It was a quick dinner, indeed, and then they had repaired up the stairs to his second-floor room. She appeared particularly eager to get there now that dinner was over, and he asked no questions. The door had not quite closed behind them when she was on him, her mouth and hands equally avid. They proceeded to peel off each other's clothes, and he was delighted when her breasts flowed into his hands. They were especially large, with smooth, heavy undersides and wide, brown nipples. He cupped them, hefted them, then leaned over and lifted them to his mouth so he could suck her nipples, which were as hard as pebbles but as big as grapes.

Her hands snaked between them, and she gasped

when she took his rigid penis into both hands. "My God . . ." she said, falling to her knees before him. "It's so pretty, so smooth, so hot . . ." she cooed, and then he was in her mouth and she was sucking him anxiously and with obvious relish. She wet him thoroughly, noisily, while cupping his heavy sack in her hands, and when she had him on the brink of exploding he reached for her, lifted her, and deposited her on the bed.

She lifted her knees and spread her thighs for him and he drove himself home, gasping as her heat surrounded him. Once he was inside she closed her legs around him and raked his back with her nails while he took her in long, easy strokes, and then quickened his tempo. She emitted little explosions of air into his ear each time he thrust his hips at her, and when her time came she signaled it with a high, keening sound that made his ears ring, but he only noticed it for a moment, and then he was discharging inside of her, and it seemed as if he would never stop. . . .

Watching her stretch in her sleep made him hard again, and he abandoned looking at the moon and thinking of the gold and went back to the bed to join her. He lay down beside her, and her hand instantly took him captive, stroking him.

"You little minx," he said, his mouth against her neck, "you weren't asleep, after all."

"I was," she said, "but then I woke up and saw you watching me."

"So you put on a performance for me, eh?" he asked, his hand sliding down over her belly until he found her, wet and waiting.

"It worked, didn't it?" she whispered. "You stopped

looking out the window and came to me. What were you looking at, out there?''

He slid a finger into her and felt her start, and then relax as he stroked her.

"Just the moon," he said. "I was thinking that when it's full the way it is tonight it hangs in the sky like a big, shimmering pearl. I was thinking how beautiful it was, until I turned and looked at you. You make the moon envious. . . ."

"Oooh," she said, as his thumb found her clitoris, "you know just what to say, don't you Canyon O'Grady. Oh, my, and what to do!"

"I hope so," he said, moving his mouth over her breasts, sliding a leg over her. He slid his hand free of her and replaced it with his cock, which was now fully hard and eager for her heat, again. . . .

2

In the morning Canyon and Lisa had breakfast together in the hotel dining room and got better acquainted. Not much of their time together in his room had been spent on conversation. There were just too many distractions.

"What brings you to New Orleans?" she asked.

"Oh," he said, having already decided on his lie, "I was looking for a pearl moon, a generous dealer, and a beautiful woman, and guess what? First night here I found all three."

She smiled, touched his hand, and his ankle with the toe of her boot.

"Canyon O'Grady, you'll kiss that Blarney stone once too often in your lifetime."

"Well, I haven't yet," he said, taking her hand in his, "so I suppose I'll just keep testing it. What brought you here?"

In point of fact, the gold could have brought her here. He knew there were going to be others looking for it, and why not a woman. Although there seemed nothing particularly southern about her, she could have been there seeking the gold for herself. There was no reason to believe that the United States Government and some fanatics from the South were the only ones looking for it. If the word was out on this gold—and apparently it had gotten out, somehow—then anyone could be looking for it, and he had to look at everyone as potential opponents.

"I like to travel," she said simply, reclaiming her hand so she could use it to lift her coffee to her lips, "and this was my next step. It was as simple as that."

"Are you well traveled?" he asked.

"Particularly well traveled," she said. "I've seen Europe and South America, but I much prefer to be home."

"And where is home?"

"I was talking about America, dear," she said. "It's all my home."

"Yes," he said, "but where were you born?"

"Ah," she said, "that. I was born in Georgia."

He frowned.

"I see you've noticed the lack of an accent," she said. "Well, I've worked very hard to get rid of it."

"Why?"

"People have a preset idea of what a southern belle is supposed to be like," she said, "and it doesn't fit me."

O'Grady thought he would have to agree with that.

"Of course," she said, laying the accent on very thick, "thaht doesn't mean ah won't use it when ah cahn, y'all."

"I imagine it might come in handy when you're playing cards," he said. "Speaking of which, how did you do last night?"

"I did very well," she said. "And you?"

"I won," he said, but didn't say how much. "Actually, I much preferred what came after."

"You're a sweet man, Canyon," she said. She

16

reached across the table again and rubbed the back of his hand. "I have to go."

"So soon?"

"I have some things I have to do," she said, standing up. She put her napkin on the table, moved to his side of the table, leaned over, and gave him a lingering kiss that had the other diners in the room enthralled. After the kiss she licked his mouth and said, "See you later?"

"I'll be here," he said.

"Bye," she said and left the room with quick, athletic strides that had the men in the room following her all the way. When she was gone they looked at O'Grady with envy, while the women in the room looked at him in an entirely different way.

He called the waiter over, paid the check, and left, taking the eyes of the female diners with him. Once Canyon *and* Lisa were gone from the room everyone went back to paying attention either to whom they were with, or to what they were eating.

Actually O'Grady wasn't really sorry that Lisa had to leave, because he had some things of his own he had to do. For one, he had to send a telegraph message to Washington to let Rufus Wheeler know that he was there and on the job. He'd arrived late in the afternoon of the previous day and had not had a chance to do so. He got directions to the nearest telegraph office from the desk clerk and took care of that little chore first.

O'Grady was staying at the St. Charles Hotel, which was in the heart of the American Quarter, on the corners of St. Charles and Common streets. The splendor of the St. Charles was second perhaps only to that of the older St. Louis Hotel, which was located in the center of the French Quarter. It was in the French Quarter that O'Grady had a preset meeting that evening, but what he wanted to do today, after he sent the telegram, was go and take a look at the area in the daylight, so it wouldn't be entirely strange to him when he went there after dark.

O'Grady had done some reading on the train about the history of New Orleans. It was founded in 1718 by a Canadian explorer named Sieur de Bienville, who named it *Nouvelle-Orleans* after the French regent, the Duke of Orleans. Since then the province had belonged either to the French or the Spanish until 1803 when General James Wilkinson and W.C.C. Clairborne, the Governor of the Mississippi Territory, marched in with troops from Ohio, Kentucky, and Tennessee and took possession of it in the name of the United States. Clairborne later became the first Governor of Louisiana.

O'Grady was supposed to meet a man named Anton LeClerc in the French Quarter, near the St. Louis Cathedral. In the center of the French Quarter was a square called Jackson Square. It had originally been called *Place d'Arms,* but after the War of 1812 it was changed to honor the man who commanded the American forces in the Battle of New Orleans.

Very near Jackson Square was another, smaller square on which the St. Louis Cathedral stood. It was in this square that O'Grady was to meet LeClerc. He saw now that it would be fairly dark there, as the area was not well lighted. Tonight he would be even more grateful for the light of the full moon, for it would keep him from risking this meeting in all but total blackness.

O'Grady spent the afternoon walking the area, taking in Canal, Esplanade, and Rampart streets, which bordered the Quarter along with the river, and then walking through the square to the very center, to take in the majesty of the St. Louis Hotel. While the structure of the St. Louis could not quite match that of the St. Charles, with its Corinthian portico and huge dome, O'Grady understood that the older St. Louis was considered New Orleans's finest hotel, while the St. Charles was thought to be its only rival.

What O'Grady did not know was that while there was little difference between the actual services of the two great hotels, the St. Louis—in the heart of the French Quarter and staunchly supported by the Creoles—was the center of the city's social life.

O'Grady returned to his own hotel in the American Quarter late in the afternoon and had a late lunch in the dining room. While the food at breakfast had been excellent, it paled in comparison to the lunch. He could only imagine what dinner would be like, but he was planning a late dinner, after his meeting with LeClerc. He preferred not to allow the impending meeting to interfere with his dinner, and so he would take it afterward, possibly in the company of Lisa Carlson.

Over lunch he thought about LeClerc. He did not know the man, in fact knew nothing about him, but the name had been given him by Wheeler as his contact in the city. It was LeClerc who was supposed to tell him what he needed to know to locate the gold. Was it, he wondered, actually physically buried somewhere, or could it have been hidden beneath the floor or in the walls of a building—a home, a church, perhaps the cathedral itself? Or one of the hotels? He understood that the St. Charles had burned down in

1851. Could someone have anticipated the need for the gold back then, and hid it when the hotel was rebuilt? Wouldn't it be ironic if the gold was hidden right in the hotel where he was staying?

Wouldn't that be *convenient*?

3

After dark O'Grady took a cab to Jackson Square.
From there he walked to the square near St. Louis
Cathedral. He knew LeClerc's name and little else
about the man. He'd been given a physical description,
but there was nothing remarkable about it. It could
have fit almost anyone.

There were streets in the French Quarter that were
alive with light and activity at this time of night. In
fact, there were many streets like that, with clubs, and
saloons, music houses, theaters, bordellos, and street
whores. The square near the cathedral, however, was
dark and quiet. O'Grady would have to assume the
only reason a man would be there would be to meet
him, or rob him.

Checking his gun, to make sure it was loose in his
holster, he entered the square and walked toward St.
Louis Cathedral. The square was lit by the full moon
on this last night that it would be full. The only sound
he heard was his own footsteps on the cobblestoned
street. The night had grown cold, and in fact there was
mist in the air. It was either raining, or it was simply
mist coming in off the nearby Mississippi. Being this
close to the river O'Grady wished he had time to spend
on a riverboat since the last time he'd been on one he

had ended up working with his old friend Skye Fargo, the Trailsman. He hadn't seen Fargo in quite a long time. He wondered what the man was doing right at that moment? Probably in a warm bed with an equally warm lass. That made him think about Lisa Carlson. He had been surprised not to see her in the hotel before he left. Surely she'd be in the casino when he returned. Perhaps they would re-create last night.

He continued walking toward the great hulk of the cathedral. He didn't know if he was to be approached in the square, or within the shadows of the cathedral. Once he reached the building even the light of the full moon would do him no good, blocked out by the great stone walls. It was at times like this, when it was cold and dangerous, that he wondered why he wasn't in some other business. Ah, but in what other business would he find such danger, the kind that made him feel so alive? The closer to death he found himself, the more alive he felt. He could never have gone through life as a tradesman, a merchant, a traveling drummer, a farmer, or a politician for that matter. No, never a politician. He'd seen too many of their kind in Washington. He liked the city of Washington, but it would have been an even better place if they had got rid of all the politicians. If that happened, though, then who would run the country? The people? If the people started running the country, wouldn't that just turn them into politicians?

Enough of that, he thought. He reached the shadows thrown by the cathedral and thought he saw something. The glowing tip of a cigarette, or a cigar perhaps?

"Hello?" he called out.

No answer.

He saw it again, glowing and then dying, and walked in that direction. As he drew closer he saw not only the glow, but the silhouette, darker against dark, of a man lounging against the wall.

"LeClerc?"

"Monsieur?" a voice returned from the dark. "Are you he who I am to meet?"

"Why else would I be here?" O'Grady asked, coming closer. He hunched his shoulders against the mist and the chill. Narrowing his eyes he could see that LeClerc was smaller than he, possibly only about five eight or nine. From his voice he sounded neither young nor old, probably middle-aged.

"I cannot see you," LeClerc said. "You were described to me, but I cannot see you."

"Whose fault is that?" O'Grady asked. "You picked the place. Let's move out into the moonlight."

"No," LeClerc said. He threw his cigarette down to the ground, where it showered sparks before dying. "Not in the light. It is not safe."

"And the darkness is?"

"I like the dark," LeClerc said. "I feel safe in the dark."

"Well, fine," O'Grady said. "Tell me what I came to hear and I'll leave you to it."

The man hesitated, then said, "The gold."

"Yes," O'Grady said, "the gold. Where is it?"

"There are others seeking it as well," LeClerc said. "You must be careful."

"I hardly need to be told that, monsieur," O'Grady said. "Just tell me what I came to be told."

"Where the gold is? Eh? Is that what you want to know?" LeClerc said.

"That's it."

"And what, then, is in it for me?"

"I don't know," O'Grady said. "That's not my department. You'll have to take that up with others."

"Why not with you?" LeClerc asked. "Why not you and I, monsieur. We could share it."

"If you know where it is," O'Grady asked, wondering if anyone else had asked him this, "why don't you just take it for yourself? Why offer it to the government?"

"It is a dangerous thing, to retrieve this gold," the Frenchman said. "It takes a dangerous man. I knew the government would send me such a man."

O'Grady was starting to get the idea. LeClerc figured he'd be able to buy whoever Washington sent with a share of the gold. In effect, LeClerc had induced the government to send him his "dangerous" man.

"I'm afraid they sent you the wrong man for the job, if that's what you have in mind," O'Grady said, but he bit his tongue as soon as the words were out of his mouth. Why not let the man think he could be bought, at least until they had recovered the gold?

"Really?" LeClerc said. O'Grady was sure that if he could see the man's face there would be a crafty expression there. He could hear it in the man's voice. "Monsieur, you have never *seen* so much gold. A small portion would make you a rich man for life. I am offering you *half.*"

O'Grady hesitated, then, playing it to the hilt said, "Half?" in what he hoped was just the right tone of voice.

Apparently it was. A chuckle came out of the darkness from the Frenchman, and then he said, "*Oui,* monsieur, half, more gold than you ever dreamed of."

"All right, LeClerc," he said, after a moment, "then where is it?"

"Ah," LeClerc said, "would I not be foolish to simply tell you? Once you know where it is, why would you need me? After all, you are a dangerous man, are you not?"

"If you say so," O'Grady said. "All right, then, how do you propose we go about this?"

"We will go and get the gold together," LeClerc said.

"Tonight?"

"*Oui,*" the man said, pushing away from the wall, "tonight. We can go—"

"Quiet," O'Grady hissed.

"Wha—"

"Shh," O'Grady said, hushing the man again.

The red-haired agent was sure he had heard something, possibly footsteps, or not so much footsteps as a foot scraping the ground. Someone was nearby, trying to move quietly, and managed to drag his foot once.

"Someone is here?" LeClerc said, sounding frightened. "You were followed?"

"Or you," O'Grady said.

"We must flee," LeClerc said.

"No," O'Grady said. "If you run you'll make a perfect target—"

"No," LeClerc said, "we cannot wait."

He started to push past O'Grady, who grabbed for him, but then there was a shot. O'Grady was so close to LeClerc he actually felt the bullet enter the man's body. LeClerc grunted and sagged against the side of the building, then slid to the ground.

O'Grady had no time to check the man. He was

diving even as another shot sounded, and then a third. Both of those bullets smacked into the wall, and then he was on the wet ground, rolling, pulling his gun free. He came up on his knees, the gun extended out in front of him toward the square, where he thought the shots must have come from. There were no further shots, but he could hear the sound of retreating footsteps.

He was torn for the moment between checking LeClerc and chasing the shooter. He finally decided to give chase, even though all he had to go on were the sound of the running feet. He started running, trying to keep the footsteps within earshot, hoping that the shooter did not have an accomplice.

Holding his gun in his hand, he ran out into the moonlight and across the square. He stopped for a moment to locate the footsteps again, his own footsteps drowning out those of the shooter. Finding them he took off once again, running now toward Jackson Square. Once they reached the center of the French Quarter, which was bound to be a flurry of activity, it was doubtful he'd be able to catch up to the shooter. Even this much of a chase was probably fruitless, but he wasn't willing to give up quite yet. After all, someone had just tried to kill him. That was not the kind of thing Canyon O'Grady took lightly.

4

Once he tracked the man through Jackson Square,
O'Grady didn't know what street he was on, but it was
lighted and busy. Light from windows illuminated the
way, and he was able to see ahead of him. What he
was not able to see was a running man, nor could he
track the man by listening for his footsteps anymore
because there was too much noise from the saloons.
His first inclination was to give up and go back to the
cathedral, but instead he continued walking.

He was accosted more than once by street whores
but brushed them off abruptly until one refused to be
brushed off. "Don't tell me," she said, "let me guess.
You're not lookin' for a woman, are you? You're
lookin' for a man, ain't ya?"

O'Grady stopped and turned to look at the woman.
She was a blowsy redhead with full, pale breasts that
were spilling out of her dress. She had a beauty mark
on her right cheek that she could not have been born
with, and her perfume was worn so thick that it was
almost making his eyes tear. In spite of all this, beneath all the makeup, he thought she was probably
fairly attractive, though somewhat middle-aged.

"That's right, miss," he said, "a running man."

"I thought as much," she said.

"Did you see him?"

"Well, I saw a running man who appeared to have the dogs of hell on his tail."

"Which way did he go?"

"Now, darlin'," she said, putting her hands on her hips and swaying from side to side so that her breasts jiggled, "do I look like I'm out here givin' it away?"

He frowned, but took five dollars from his pocket and gave it to her. Her eyes widened, and it was obvious that this was much more than she had hoped for. It disappeared from his fingers and into her cleavage in the wink of an eye.

"Two doors ahead of you," she said, "is the Blue Goose Tavern and Saloon," she said. "He went in there."

"I thank you, ma'am," O'Grady said, gallantly.

"You want to thank me?" she asked. "Come back later and save me from havin' to service some fat merchant who is stealing a night away from his even fatter wife."

He smiled and said, "I might just take you up on that, miss."

"And stop callin' me miss," she said. "Kelly is my name. Remember it. We redheads have to stick together, now don't we?"

"That we do, Kelly," he said. "Thanks for the information."

"Don't thank me," she said, "you paid for it. What'd he do, anyway, this man you're chasin'?"

"Tried to kill me," he said, "and did kill another fella I was standing with."

"That so? No wonder he wouldn't give me a tumble. Fella as ugly as him, I figured he'd have to pay for it.

Now you, on the other hand, you come back later and I'll do you for free, lover.''

"Again," he said, touching the brim of his hat, "I'll keep it in mind. I'll have to be going if I'm going to catch up with him."

"Good luck."

He nodded, walked two doors down, and peered inside the Blue Goose Tavern and Saloon. It was wall to wall with men *and* women, and the air was thick with smoke. If his man had gone in there he was going to be hell to find, especially since he didn't know what he looked like.

He had one thing working in his favor, though, and that was that the shooter probably did know what *he* looked like. If the man saw him, he might give himself away. He only hoped that he would do so while giving ample warning, so that the redhaired agent would be able to spot him before being shot dead himself.

He pushed through the batwing doors and entered the tavern, holstering his gun. He did not want to draw undue attention to himself by brandishing the weapon openly. Inside, the noise was deafening enough with chatter when someone decided to add to it by playing the piano, badly.

O'Grady pushed through the crowd, staring hard into the faces of the men he passed. He did have something of a description to go by. The whore had said that the man was ugly, and although there were plenty who could go by that description, there were enough that could be discounted as well.

When he reached the bar the bartender asked what he wanted and he ordered a beer. He was tall enough to continue to rake the room with his eyes, seeing above the heads of most of the people in the room.

Far in the back he saw something promising. An ugly face looked his way while trying to seem not to be. The man was indeed ugly, with a huge nose and jutting chin, and he was skulking, trying to blend in with the crowd.

When the bartender brought the beer O'Grady paid for it, took a hasty swig, and then began to push through the crowd toward the ugly man. He wasn't sure this was his prey, but there was one sure way to find out, and that was to ask.

It turned out he didn't have to ask. As he started over the man's eyes widened and he turned, trying to flee through the crowd.

"Hold it!" O'Grady shouted, but there was little chance that the man heard, and even smaller chance that he would have stopped even if he had. O'Grady started to push harder through the crowd.

"What's the rush, big fella?" a woman asked him. She was nothing special to look at, but he spoke to her.

"Is there a back door in this place?"

"Sure is," she said, lifting her arm above the crowd so that the flesh of her upper arm jiggled as she pointed. "It's in the back, whataya know?"

"Thanks."

Obviously the ugly man was headed that way, and he was sure to get there first. O'Grady continued to push even as he saw his prey disappear through a doorway. Pushing once again he finally came up against someone who did not take kindly to it.

"Hey, who are you pushin'?" a heavyset man asked. He was shorter than O'Grady, but built much lower to the ground and would not budge willingly.

Having no time to waste O'Grady took out his gun and pressed the barrel beneath the man's chin.

"Either move or find your brains on the ceiling," he said.

"Take it easy, friend," the man said, "I'm moving," and proceeded to do so quickly.

When he finally reached the door himself Canyon drew his gun and went through it in a crouch. He found himself in a hallway alone. He followed the hallway to a closed door, which led outside. As he reached it he saw that it was not closed, but ajar. He kicked it open with one foot and went through it low and fast. There was a shot, and he heard the bullet whiz overhead.

It was darker back here than in the front, and it took a moment for his eyes to adjust. He saw he was in an alley. There was not a second shot, and once again he found himself chasing after retreating footsteps.

He came out of the alley onto another street, not quite so busy or lighted as the other. The problem was that he no longer heard running footsteps and didn't know whether to go right or left. Either way would lead to a more busy street where a fleeing man could once again have his choice of places to duck into.

Having to make some sort of decision or lose the man through indecision he turned right and ran to the corner. As he turned it he saw another lighted and busy street, but this time there were no whores to point him in the right direction. He turned to look behind him, then ahead of him. Once again he had the choice of two directions and made it hastily.

He started forward, peering into windows and doors, but before long he had to admit that had had finally lost the shooter. There was something else he had to admit—he had gotten himself so turned around he did not know how to get back to the cathedral. He began to look around for someone who could give him directions.

When O'Grady returned to the cathedral it became apparent that the earlier shots had been noticed by someone, who had then summoned a policeman. That policeman had summoned two others, so that when the agent returned to the scene he found three policemen crowded around the body of the man he knew as LeClerc.

As he approached one of the uniformed policemen noticed him and nudged the others. All three turned and although he couldn't make their features out clearly, he had the impression that they were all fairly young.

"Who're you?" one of them demanded. His voice almost squeaked from nervousness.

"My name's O'Grady."

"Do you know anything about this?"

He could have lied, but then he'd have to explain what he was doing there now. He decided a half truth was in order. "Not much, I'm afraid," he said. "I was passing and heard the shots. When I ran over he was lying on the ground."

"And what did you do?" the same policeman asked. He seemed to be the spokesman.

"I heard someone running across the square, so I took up the chase."

"And?"

"I lost him."

"And why did you come back?"

"Why to see how he was," O'Grady said. "If he was alive, I was going to try to help him. Is he?"

"Is he what?"

"Alive," O'Grady said, "is he alive?"

"No," the policeman said, "he's dead."

The three policemen exchanged glances, and then the spokesman produced his gun with a quick, almost convulsive move and said, "Mister, I think my boss is going to have some more questions for you."

"There's no need for the gun," O'Grady said. "I'll answer all the questions you have."

"That's good," the man said, "that's real good, because my boss likes to ask a lot of questions. We'll take your gun now."

O'Grady hesitated a moment, but when the other two policemen also drew their guns nervously he said, "All right, just stay calm." He hoped he'd be able to give them his gun without getting shot himself.

5

The young policeman's boss turned out to be Inspector George Quitman, and the man did indeed have a lot of questions.

O'Grady was forced to wait at the scene while one of the policemen went for help. Responding to his call was the inspector, as well as some men with a wagon to remove the body.

"Get him into the light," Inspector Quitman instructed. "I want to see his face."

"I have a lamp, Inspector," one of the men on the wagon said. The body was in the back of the wagon by this time, so the lamp was lit and then one of the policemen held it while the inspector lifted the dead man's head and looked at his face.

"LeClerc," he said. "Anton LeClerc." He retained his hold on the dead man's head and called out to one of the policemen, "Bring the other one over here."

"Let's go," one of the young policemen said, prodding O'Grady, who decided to suffer the prodding, for the moment.

"O'Grady, was it?" Inspector Quitman asked.

"That's right."

"Take a look at this man's face, please."

O'Grady looked at the face and had no problem telling the inspector that he had never seen the man before in his life.

"You don't know him?"

"That's what I said," O'Grady said.

"No," Quitman said, letting the dead man's head drop so that it made a knocking sound on the bottom of the wagon when it hit. "No, that's not what you said. You said you had never seen him before in your life."

"That's the same thing."

"I see we're going to be talking for some time tonight, Mr. O'Grady," Quitman said. "You'll find that I am a firm believer in plain talk. I do not take kindly to ambiguous language."

"Really?"

"If you want me to understand what you're saying, you had better say it plain," Quitman said.

At that moment another wagon arrived. Quitman turned to look at it, then looked at O'Grady and said, "Your ride is here. I will see you at headquarters when I've finished here."

"Inspector," O'Grady said, "do you have any idea how long this is going to take?"

Inspector Quitman smiled grimly at O'Grady and said, "No."

O'Grady was taken to police headquarters where he was put in a room with a table and two chairs. He was left there alone. At one point he rose and opened the door, only to have his way barred by a uniformed police officer, a bigger, more experienced officer than he had encountered in the square by the cathedral.

"How about some coffee?" he asked.

35

The man hesitated, then said, "I'll see to it."

"Thank you."

The coffee arrived about fifteen minutes later, a pot and one cup. O'Grady was almost finished with the entire pot when Inspector Quitman finally arrived.

Quitman left the door open, and when he spotted the pot he turned to the policeman outside the door and said, "Get another pot of coffee and some food."

"Yes, sir."

With that Quitman closed the door. He removed his jacket, hung it over the back of the empty chair, and sat opposite O'Grady. "Anton LeClerc is no loss," he said, "but I don't like having men killed in my jurisdiction."

"Can't say I blame you for that."

"What hotel are you staying at?"

"The St. Charles."

Quitman raised one eyebrow and said, "Expensive."

"Somewhat."

"What is it you do for a living that you can afford to stay in the St. Charles Hotel?"

"I'm a gambler," O'Grady said, falling back on an old dodge. It usually explained how he made a living, and why he "traveled" so much.

"Why doesn't that surprise me?" Quitman asked. O'Grady knew the question did not call for an answer, so he didn't offer one.

The door opened and the older police officer entered with a fresh pot of coffee. He put it on the table and then addressed his superior. "The food will be here soon, Inspector."

"Very good, Russell," Quitman said. "Will you

send someone to the St. Charles Hotel to make some inquiries about Mr. O'Grady?"

"Yes, sir."

"Oh, and make sure there are utensils and plates enough for two, will you? Mr. O'Grady will be dining with us tonight." He looked at O'Grady and said, "You don't mind, do you?"

"As a matter of fact," O'Grady said, "I haven't eaten tonight."

"It won't be anything fancy, I'm afraid."

"Anything will do."

"Fine," Quitman said. "Now that we have that out of the way, would you care to tell me what you were doing in the square by St. Louis Cathedral?"

"Sightseeing."

Quitman took a deep breath and let it out slowly, then said, "I can see that we are going to be here a long time, aren't we?"

For the most part O'Grady answered the inspector's questions honestly. The only thing he didn't tell the inspector was what he really did for a living, what he was really doing in New Orleans, and what he was really doing near St. Louis Cathedral. Unfortunately the points the inspector seemed to be dwelling on were what he was doing in New Orleans and specifically what he was doing near the cathedral.

"Let's go over this again, Mr. O'Grady," the inspector said.

On the table in front of them was a tray strewn with empty serving plates. Pushed to one side were the utensils, bowls, and plates they had eaten from. They had been brought some gumbo, followed by some jambalaya from a nearby restaurant. O'Grady was surprised at how good the food was.

"Your name is Canyon O'Grady."

"Correct."

"I don't have a problem with that," Quitman said. "You're a gambler."

"Right."

"I also don't have a problem with that," the policeman said. "Now, what were you doing in the square near St. Louis Cathedral tonight?"

"Sightseeing."

"Now see," Quitman said, "I *do* have a problem with that."

"I can't imagine why."

"Well, for one thing," Quitman said, "you don't strike me as the sightseeing type, and for another I would think you would want to see the cathedral in the light of day."

"I did," O'Grady said. "I saw it this afternoon in the daylight, and I wanted to see it tonight by moonlight. You *have* noticed that the moon has been full the last two nights?"

"Yes, I have noticed," Quitman said, "but I would rather spend my time beneath a moon like that with a pretty lady, and not looking at the cathedral."

O'Grady could believe that. Even he had to admit that the inspector—tall, broad-shouldered, fortyish—was a handsome man. He probably spent a lot of time looking at the moon with pretty ladies.

"Let's go back to the actual shooting," Quitman said.

"We've gone over it a dozen times."

"Let's go over it again," the inspector said. "You were looking at the cathedral spire, right?"

"Correct."

"And you heard a shot."

"I heard three shots," O'Grady said, because there was one bullet in LeClerc and two bullet holes in the wall of the cathedral.

"Oh, that's right," Quitman said, "you did say that, didn't you? Three shots."

"Right."

"And you ran around to the side of the cathedral to see what had happened."

"Right again."

"You saw a man on the ground and heard someone running."

"Yes."

"Why did you chase him? Why didn't you stay with the injured man or summon help?"

"I don't know," O'Grady said. "My first instinct was to run after the man who had done the shooting. I also thought I'd be able to find help in a more populated area."

"What if LeClerc was still alive?" Quitman said. "What if by running off you actually left him to die."

"If that's the case, then I'm truly sorry," O'Grady said, "but I can't go back and do it again, and even if I were able to do so, I don't know that I would do it any differently."

"Well," Quitman said, "you may not do it differently, but you certainly are telling it the same way every time."

"Because that's the way it happened."

"Yes, but in my experience, even when someone has to repeat a story again and again, there are usually some small differences. In your case, you've told the story each and every time in exactly the same way. Do you know what that makes me think?''

"No, Inspector," O'Grady said, "I don't know what that makes you think, but I'm sure you're going to tell me."

"It makes me think that maybe, just maybe, you've rehearsed this little story."

"And why would I do that?"

"So that we won't think that *you* killed Anton LeClerc," Quitman said.

"And why would I kill a man I don't even know?" O'Grady asked.

"That's right," Quitman said, snapping his fingers, "you did say that, didn't you? That you didn't know LeClerc?"

"I've only been in New Orleans for a couple of days, Inspector," O'Grady said. "How would I have met him?"

"I don't know," Russell said. "I'm just asking questions here, O'Grady, trying to find out as much as I can."

"The simple fact is I didn't know the man, and I have no idea who shot him. Also, I chased after the man who shot him."

"Ah, there's something we haven't explored," Quitman said. O'Grady didn't like the way he used the word *explored*, as if this was going to take the other half of the night.

"What's that?"

"What did the man look like?" Quitman asked. "The man who shot LeClerc?"

"I don't know," O'Grady said. "I never saw him."

"Wait a minute," Quitman said. "I'm a little confused here. Didn't you just say you chased him?"

"I said I chased *after* him," O'Grady said.

"Oh, that's right," Quitman said, "you did say that. And wasn't I the one who said we had to talk plain? Of course, you chased after him without ever having seen him. Is that right?"

"That's correct."

"Never even saw him from behind?"

"I heard footsteps, running," O'Grady said, "and I ran in that direction."

"For how long?" Quitman asked.

"For how long, what?"

"How long did you continue to run after the sound of the footsteps?"

"For as long as I could hear them," O'Grady said. "I ran through Jackson Square to the street beyond it."

"What street was that?"

"I don't know, Inspector," O'Grady said. "The fact is I got all turned around and had to ask directions to get back to the cathedral."

"I see," Quitman said. He paused now, took out a cigar, and made a show of lighting it until he had it going the way he wanted, frowning the whole time as if he was deep in thought. In that moment Inspector Quitman reminded O'Grady of Rufus Wheeler.

"I see," Quitman said again, around the cigar. "Was this a busy street?"

"Very busy," O'Grady said.

"So then somebody probably saw you, and maybe even saw the man you were chasing."

"Maybe," O'Grady agreed.

"Excellent, excellent," Quitman said. "I'll put men on the streets and we'll probably come up with someone who saw both of you."

"Inspector," O'Grady said, "you don't really think that I shot LeClerc, do you? Then ran off and came back later to talk to three policeman?"

Quitman spread his hands helplessly and said, "As I said before, Mr. O'Grady, I'm just asking questions, trying to get the whole picture."

"Well," O'Grady asked, "just how much longer do you think it will be before you have the whole picture, Inspector?"

"Oh, quite a while, I expect, Mr. O'Grady," Quitman said, "quite a while—"

"Jesus—"

"—but you can go now."

It was an obvious dismissal, but so abrupt that it surprised O'Grady. "I can go?"

"Yes," Quitman said. "It will take more than tonight for me to finally get the whole picture. In fact I may need to call upon you again in the near future."

"Well . . . that's fine," O'Grady said, standing up. "I'm anxious to help, Inspector."

"Well, that's fine," Quitman said. "That means you won't be leaving the city any time soon?"

"No, sir," O'Grady said, thinking about that cache of gold he had to find now without a clue, "not any time real soon."

6

When O'Grady left the police station he had a coach take him back to the St. Charles Hotel. The casino was still in action, but it certainly was not in full swing. Some of the tables were closed and covered, many of the guests had gone to bed, and he didn't see Lisa Carlson anywhere, which was actually just as well. He was exhausted from the evening's happenings, even more so from Inspector Quitman's relentless questioning than from all the running he had done.

He stopped at the bar, had a quick shot of whiskey, and then went up to his room. He had to admit he wasn't hungry. Quitman had fed him and fed him quite well.

When he opened the door to his room he almost expected to find Lisa there in his bed waiting for him, but apparently she was neither that forward nor that anxious to see him again. In fact he couldn't really remember if they had agreed to definitely meet that night. If they had, she was bound to be angry at him for standing her up.

As he pulled off his boots he realized that whether or not Lisa Carlson was mad at him should be the least of his worries. Anton LeClerc, the man who was supposed to lead him to the hidden cache of gold, was now dead. He still had the responsibility to find the gold, only he didn't have the first clue as to where to look. In the morning he was going to have to send a telegram to Wheeler and give his superior the bad news. Maybe Wheeler would be able to come up with some more information for him, but if he didn't, O'Grady knew that the last thing the man would tell him was to forget all about it and come back to Washington. He was going to be stuck in New Orleans until either he found the gold or someone else did.

He undressed and crawled under the bed covers. He stared at the ceiling in the dark and wondered idly if LeClerc had been the actual intended target tonight, or if it had been him. He also wondered why Inspector Quitman hadn't asked that question. Was the inspector assuming that LeClerc was the target? He did not seem to O'Grady to be the kind of man who would assume anything. The inspector was obviously a very thorough man, and being thorough, he probably had someone follow O'Grady back to the hotel.

O'Grady got up out of bed and walked to the window without lighting a lamp. His room overlooked the street in front of the hotel, and he kept his eyes on the doorways across the street. If Quitman had sent someone to follow him, then he had probably told that someone to watch the hotel until morning. O'Grady didn't see any moving shadows or any glowing cigarette tips, but he was suddenly convinced that there was a policeman across the way watching the hotel, and probably watching his exact window.

Even if it was true, there was little to be done about it now. He left the window and went back to the warmth of the bed. There was little to be done about anything at the moment, and even less to be solved by lying awake thinking about it.

Having decided that, Canyon O'Grady went right to sleep and slept through until morning.

O'Grady rose at eight, pulled on his trousers and a shirt, and went downstairs to arrange for a bath. After the bath he dressed in fresh clothes and went to the dining room for breakfast.

"Good morning, sir," said the waiter who had served him each time he had eaten there, whether it had been breakfast, lunch, or dinner.

"Don't they ever let you sleep?" he asked.

"But of course, sir," the waiter said. The man was in his sixties and looked well rested enough. "What can I get for you this morning?"

O'Grady ordered eggs and sausage, biscuits, and coffee.

"And some grits?" the waiter asked. He had asked that each time at breakfast.

"No," O'Grady answered, as he had before, "no grits. Thank you."

"Very well, sir."

The coffee came immediately and the food soon after. O'Grady was just about to start eating when he saw Inspector George Quitman enter the dining room. The policeman looked around, saw him, and walked over.

"Do you mind if I join you?" Quitman asked.

"Why not?" O'Grady said. "After all, you bought me dinner, didn't you?"

"Yes," Quitman said, sitting, "I suppose I did, didn't I?"

The waiter automatically brought over another cup

and then greeted the inspector by name. "What can I get for you, sir?"

"Nothing, Louis," Quitman said. "Just coffee will be fine."

"As you wish, sir."

"I'm impressed," O'Grady said. "Does a waiter over at the St. Louis also know you by sight?"

"Only if I've arrested him," Quitman said.

"You arrested Louis once?" O'Grady asked in surprise.

"Not once," Quitman said. "Three times, the last time being a dozen or so years ago. It's all old news."

"What did you arrest him for?"

Quitman smiled over his coffee cup and said, "I'm afraid you'll have to ask Louis that question."

"Well then," O'Grady said, "to what do I owe this pleasure? Surely you didn't forget to ask me any questions last night."

"Actually I didn't forget," Quitman said, "but there were a few I thought of after you left. Do you mind?"

"Like I said last night, Inspector," O'Grady replied, "I want to help."

"Yes," Quitman said, "you did say that last night, didn't you?"

"Yes," O'Grady said, "I did, and I think in those exact words."

If Quitman noticed that O'Grady was being sarcastic he let it pass. "Tell me something, Mr. O'Grady," Quitman said, "do you think that those shots last night could have been meant for you?"

If O'Grady hadn't been on his guard the question would have caught him. Even if he had answered no, he had to remember that his story was that he was nowhere near LeClerc when the shots were fired.

"Hardly, Inspector," he said. "Remember, I was in front of the cathedral when the shots were fired, and LeClerc was on the side. Someone would have had to be a very poor shot to miss me by that much."

"A good point, Mr. O'Grady," Quitman said, "A very good point. Please, don't let me keep you from your breakfast."

The food had grown cold by this time, but O'Grady proceeded to eat it, anyway.

"I don't know what possessed me to ask that question," Quitman said.

"It's very simple," O'Grady said, buttering a cool biscuit. "You don't believe me."

"Oh, how could I not believe you?" Quitman asked. "I mean, what reason would you have to lie to a policeman?"

"Inspector," O'Grady said, "why is it you have the distinct opinion that everyone lies to you?"

"Do I?" Quitman asked, as if taken aback by the question. "You know, I probably do. That's terrible! I mean, how could I be so cynical?"

"Maybe it comes from being a policeman for so many years," O'Grady said. "Do you think?"

"You know," Quitman said, "you might be right."

"Is there anything else I can help you with?" O'Grady asked.

"Uh, no, as a matter of fact that seems to be the only other question I had for you," Quitman said, rising.

"Then let me ask you one."

"Go ahead."

"Are you going to have me followed everywhere I go from now until you find LeClerc's killer?"

"For that long?" Quitman asked. "My goodness, no. That could take forever."

"Ah . . ."

"No," Quitman went on, smiling, "I'm only going to have you followed for as long as you are in New Orleans. Enjoy your breakfast, Mr. O'Grady."

7

O'Grady was finishing off his breakfast with more coffee when Lisa Carlson walked into the dining room. He needed wonder no longer whether she was angry with him or not. He knew she saw him, and yet she walked to another table without so much as glancing his way.

O'Grady sighed, called Louis over and paid his check. Then he told Louis that Miss Carlson would not be paying for her own breakfast. "No matter what happens," he added.

"As you say, sir," Louis said.

O'Grady got up from his table and walked over to Lisa's. "Good morning," he said.

She looked up at him and acted as if she hadn't noticed him earlier. "Oh, good morning," she said. "I didn't see you."

"Lisa," he said, "you couldn't help but see me. You didn't want to see me."

"Oh, well," she said, looking directly at him now, "I guess it was last night that I wanted to see you and not this morning."

"I can explain about last night."

"Can you?" she asked. "Did you get a better offer?"

"Not a better offer," he said, "just a different one."

"I'll bet."

"From the police."

"The police?"

"Can I sit down and explain . . . please?"

She studied him for a moment, then said, "All right . . . but this better be good."

He sat across from her and told her what had happened. His story was the same as the one he had given to Inspector Quitman, just on the off chance that Quitman, thorough man that he was, would end up talking to her.

"You went to look at the cathedral?" she asked. "In the dark?"

"Why does everyone find that so hard to believe?" he asked.

"I'm sorry," she said, "I didn't mean—and they kept you all night?"

"Most of the night," he said. "The policeman in charge is very thorough. By the time I got back here it was so late I didn't want to wake you."

"I wish you had," she said.

"I'm sorry," he said, "but to tell you the truth, I was also very exhausted."

She stared at him for a moment, then leaned forward and said, "You are being truthful, aren't you." Her tone said she knew that he was.

"Yes," he said, "I am."

"It must have been terrible for you."

"It wasn't so terrible," he said. "I mean, I'm not totally unused to violence."

"As a gambler?"

"Well, some people don't take kindly to losing, you know."

She reached across the table and covered his hand with hers. "You don't have to try to convince me what a man you are, Canyon," she said. "I know."

"What are you doing today?" he asked.

"Oh, I don't know," she said, sitting back. "I thought I'd do some shopping."

"Well, I have some errands to run this morning," he said, "but maybe we can have lunch later?"

"Here?"

He smiled and said, "Here is as good a place as any."

She smiled too because she was thinking the same thing. "Better than any," she said, because it was right near their rooms.

"Enjoy your breakfast," he said. He stood up, took her hand, and kissed it. "I'll see you back here at one?"

"One it is," she said.

He smiled at her and left the dining room.

The hotel had its own telegraph key, but he hadn't used it the first time he'd sent a telegram to Washington, and he didn't intend to use it now. He left the hotel and walked three blocks to the telegraph office he had used the day before. On the way he stopped briefly to look in the window of a hat shop. Using the window he was able to spot the man who was following him, the policeman Inspector Quitman had left to follow him—at least, he hoped it was a policeman. There was always the possibility that it was the man who had shot at him and LeClerc the night before.

He wondered why the man hadn't shot at him first, or had he? Had he been a terrible shot, striking Le-Clerc when he was actually aiming at O'Grady? And what about LeClerc? Had he been setting O'Grady up without knowing that he'd also be a target? Had the whole thing been a double cross all around, LeClerc trying to double-cross O'Grady, and the shooter double-crossing LeClerc? After all, LeClerc had been in no particular hurry to tell O'Grady about the gold.

He continued walking, letting the man follow him. Quitman had admitted that he was having him followed, so the man had to be a policeman. He decided to stop worrying about it. If there was someone else following him, the policeman would see him.

By the time he reached the telegraph office he had composed the message in his mind. It would make no sense to the clerk, but that didn't matter. Wheeler would know what it meant, that his only contact was dead, and he was waiting for further instructions. From the window of the telegraph office he could see a small restaurant across the street.

He gave the clerk some extra money and said, "When a reply comes I'll be in that place across the street. Will you bring it over to me?"

The clerk looked at the money in his hand and said, "Sure, mister."

"Thanks."

O'Grady left the telegraph office and crossed the street to the restaurant. Inside he asked the waitress for a table by the window, which he saw was available. She allowed him to sit there and then took his order for coffee.

"Just coffee?" she asked. She was a pretty thing and thrust her hip out when she asked, "Nothing else?"

He smiled up at her and said, "Just the coffee . . . for now."

He settled into his seat and looked out the window.

He could see the telegraph office right across the street, and a few doors down from that he saw the policeman who was following him. He had settled into the doorway of some kind of store and was watching the front of the restaurant. O'Grady didn't know if the man could see him sitting at the window, since the lower half of the window was covered with a curtain. He had the urge to wave at the man to check but decided against it.

"Here's your coffee," the waitress said, setting it in front of him.

"Thanks."

"How about a piece of cake?" she asked. She clasped her hands behind and was swinging back and forth, obviously trying to get his attention. If he didn't already have a meeting set with Lisa, the waitress wouldn't have had any trouble getting his attention. He decided to be sociable.

"What's your name?"

"Sara."

"Been working here long?"

"A couple of years."

She looked to be about twenty-four or -five.

"I won't be here much longer, though."

"Why's that?"

"I'm really an actress," she said. "I hope to get into a play at the St. Philip Theater. After that, who knows?"

"Maybe San Francisco, huh?" he said.

"Or New York," she said. "I'd love to go to either place."

"You know," he said, "you live in a beautiful city now."

"I know," she said, "but I want to see San Fran-

53

cisco and New York . . . and maybe even Europe. I want to travel all over.''

''We all do,'' he said.

''Do you travel?''

''Yes,'' he said, ''I travel quite a bit.''

''Are you an important man?''

''Why do you ask that?''

She shrugged and said, ''You look important.''

''Well, I'm not,'' he said, ''not to anybody.''

''Well . . . you could come and see me at the theater, anyway.''

''When?''

''Next week,'' she said, then added, ''if I get the part.''

''Well,'' he said, ''take my advice. Even if you *do* get the job, don't give up this job so fast.''

''Oh, once I get into the theater I'm leavin' this job for good,'' she said with conviction.

He decided to keep his advice to himself after that. ''I don't think I'll have any cake with this coffee, Sara,'' he said.

''All right,'' she said. ''I'll come and refill your cup for you in a little while.''

There were other people in the restaurant, some eating and some waiting to be served. Sara and one other girl were the only ones working, and now Sara went over to a man and a woman who were looking very impatient. At that moment two men came through the doorway, talking and laughing, but when they saw O'Grady sitting by the window they stopped and frowned.

''Hey . . .'' one of them said.

''Come on,'' the other said.

They were both in their twenties, fairly well dressed and brimming with attitudes of self importance.

"Get up," one of them said.

O'Grady looked up at them. One had muttonchops, but the other had pink cheeks that said he had shaved fairly recently. They were both frowning down at him, probably trying to intimidate him with their stares.

"Are you talking to me?" O'Grady asked.

"Yeah," Muttonchops said, "we're talkin' to you."

"Your sittin' in our seats," Pink Cheeks said.

"Your seats?"

"That's right," Muttonchops said, "that's our table. We always sit there."

"Well," O'Grady said, "just let me finish my coffee and I'll be happy to move."

"No," Muttonchops said, "we want you to move now."

O'Grady put his coffee cup down and looked up at them. At that moment Sara came walking over.

"You don't own that table, Will Kane," she said, putting her hands on her hips.

"You know we always sit there, Sara," Muttonchops said.

"Well, not today," she said. "There are plenty of other tables to be had."

"We don't want another table," Pink Cheeks said. "We want this one, and this fella is gonna get up and give it to us, ain't you?"

"Well, I'll tell you," O'Grady said, "if you boys had come in and explained the situation to me nicely and asked me to give up the table, I would have. However, since you seem to think you have some right to demand the table, I think I'll just sit here and have another cup of coffee. Sara?"

"I'll get it for you, mister," she said. She looked at the other two men and said, "Don't start no trouble in here, Will Kane."

O'Grady got the impression that Muttonchops was Will Kane.

"Never mind her," Will Kane said to the other man. He turned and looked at O'Grady. "You gettin' up friend? Or are we makin' you?"

"Lean over here," O'Grady said.

"What?"

"Lean over here and take a look out this window," O'Grady said.

"Huh?" Kane said. He leaned over and looked out the window. "Where?"

"Across the street? In that doorway over there? See that man?"

Kane frowned, then said, "Uh, yeah, I see him. So what?"

"He's a policeman."

"He is?" Kane straightened up.

"Yes, he is."

"What's he doin' over there?"

"He's following me," O'Grady said.

"What for?"

"Because I kill people."

"Huh?"

Kane looked at his friend, who stared back in disbelief.

"That is," O'Grady said, "the police think I kill people . . . but I don't . . . not really."

"Whataya mean, not really?"

Sara came with the coffeepot then and refilled O'Grady's cup.

56

"Are these boys still causing you trouble, mister?" she asked.

"Why no," O'Grady said, "quite the contrary, I was just inviting them to sit down with me and share the table."

"Is that right?" she asked.

"Uh, yeah," Will Kane said to her, "yeah, that's right."

"Sit right down, boys," O'Grady said magnanimously. "Sara, bring them a cup each and take their order. Why, I might even buy these boys their lunch."

8

The two young men, Will Kane and Paul Majors, sat and ate their lunch while staring across the table at Canyon O'Grady as though he had horns.

"Naturally," O'Grady said, "just because someone gets killed everywhere I go doesn't mean I killed them, but can you convince the police of that?"

Neither of the young men answered.

"Can you?" he demanded.

"Uh, no," Majors said.

"No, no, of course not," Will Kane said.

"That's right," O'Grady said, "of course not."

Kane turned and looked longingly out the window at the policeman across the street.

"What are you looking at?" O'Grady asked.

"Me?" Kane said when Majors prodded him with an elbow. "Oh, nothing."

"Did you hear about the murder last night?" O'Grady asked the two men.

"W-what murder?" Kane asked.

"I think I heard s-something," Majors said. "A man was killed near St. Louis Cathedral?"

"That's the one," O'Grady said. "Some coincidence, huh? Just as I get into town somebody gets killed."

O'Grady looked at their plates, which were still half full. "You boys haven't finished your lunch," O'Grady said.

"Uh, I'm not real hungry," Will Kane said.

"Me, neither."

O'Grady gave them each a hard stare and said, "You wouldn't want to make me waste my money, would you?"

"Well, actually," Kane said, pushing against Majors so he'd get up, "we really have to be getting back to work."

"R-right," Majors said. "If we get back late we're liable to get fired. Uh, thanks for the lunch, mister."

"Yeah, thanks," Kane said, and he and his friend made hastily for the door.

"Boy," Sara said, coming over, "what did you do to them?"

"I guess I scared them a little," he said, looking at her innocently.

"I guess you did," she said. "They almost ran out of here, and after I thought they were going to start something with you."

"No," he said, noticing that the telegraph agent was crossing the street toward the restaurant. "Not them. They were real nice fellas."

The agent entered the restaurant, looked around, spotted O'Grady, and came over.

"Here's your reply, mister," he said, handing it to O'Grady.

"Thanks," O'Grady said. He looked at Sara and asked, "Could I get one more cup of coffee?"

"Sure," she said, "comin' up."

As she walked away he opened the telegram and read. It said: DO THE BEST YOU CAN.

59

That was just like Rufus Wheeler. In effect he was telling Canyon O'Grady that he was on his own. Unspoken were the instructions, DON'T COME BACK WITHOUT THE GOLD.

O'Grady was standing up when Sara returned with the coffeepot.

"Change your mind?" she asked.

"I have to go," he said. "Thanks for the coffee." He gave her ten times what the coffee cost.

"Mister—"

"Keep the change," he said.

As he was going out the door she called out, "Don't forget to come and see me at the theater."

"I'll be there," he promised.

He crossed the street and started walking back in the direction of the hotel. As he approached the doorway that the policeman was in he could see Will Kane and Paul Majors talking to the man earnestly. When they saw O'Grady approaching him they started talking faster and pointing at him. As O'Grady walked past the three men he said, "Have a nice day," and kept going.

"Aren't you going to do something?" he heard Will Kane ask. O'Grady didn't hear the answer, but he knew without looking that the policeman was following him back to the hotel.

When he got back to the hotel it was twelve-thirty. He had a half an hour before he met Lisa down in the dining room. He saw no reason not to spend the rest of the day with her. He was going to need at least that long to come up with some kind of a plan. With absolutely no leads on the location of the gold, there was only one thing for him to do. He had to find someone who knew Anton LeClerc, and he had to do *that* without letting the police know he was doing it. If Inspector Quitman found out that he was looking for a friend or business acquaintance of LeClerc's, he might get it into his head that O'Grady was at the cathedral to meet LeClerc—which, of course, he was, but he didn't want Quitman to know that.

O'Grady started to his room, leaving the policeman who was following him down in the lobby. But first he stopped at the front desk. "Can I help you, sir?" the desk clerk asked.

"Yes," O'Grady said, "I'd like you to send a bellboy to my room in ten minutes. Can you do that?"

"Yes, sir, of course," the man said. "Would you like him to bring anything with him?"

"No," O'Grady said, "just make sure you send me someone who knows his way around New Orleans. Understand?"

"Oh, yes sir," the clerk said, knowingly, "I understand perfectly."

"Good."

He went up to his room to await the bellboy.

He only had to wait five minutes before there was a knock at the door. It was not a bellboy that the clerk had sent up, but a bellman. He was a bandy-legged little man of about forty-five, with steel gray hair and eyes to match.

"What's your name?" O'Grady asked, letting him in.

"Shoe," the man said, "Bill Shoe, but you can just call me Shoe. Everybody does."

"Okay, Shoe."

"I hear you want somebody who knows his way around New Orleans?"

"I want someone who knows the streets of New Orleans," O'Grady said. Shoe did not say *New* Orleans. He pronounced it like most of the locals did, "N'Orleans."

"Well, I'm your man, mister—"

"Canyon," O'Grady said, "just call me Canyon."

"All right, Canyon," Shoe said, "suppose you tell me what you're lookin' for? Gamblin'? Women? A little of both? A lot of both."

"I'll tell you what I'm looking for, Shoe," O'Grady said, "but this has to stay between you and me."

"Who would I tell?"

"It's not who you'd tell that worries me," O'Grady said, "it's who might ask you."

Shoe closed one eye, cocked his head to one side, and said, "Who might ask me?"

"The police."

"Hell," Shoe said, "I ain't told the police nothin' in forty years; I ain't about to start now. What is it we're lookin' for, Canyon?"

"I'm looking for someone who knew a man named Anton LeClerc."

Shoe took a step back, blinked and said, "That sonofabitch?"

"I guess you knew him?"

"Oh, I knew him," She said. "I knew him well enough to want to pin a medal on whoever killed him last night. It wasn't you, was it?"

"No, it wasn't me," O'Grady said, "but I was there when it happened."

"You and LeClerc weren't friends, were you?" Shoe asked.

"No," O'Grady said, "I didn't even know the man. Our meeting had been prearranged."

"By who?"

"I can't tell you that."

"Okay, then why?"

"I can't tell you that, either . . . exactly. See, LeClerc was going to help me out with something that I have to do, and now he's dead."

"And you need someone who knew what he knew, right?" Shoe asked.

"That's exactly right, Shoe," O'Grady said. "Do you think you can help me with that?"

"Well," Shoe said, scratching his head, "I can sure nose around a bit, Canyon, but it ain't gonna come cheap, ya know?"

"Oh, I know that, Shoe," O'Grady said, nodding his head. "I know that for sure."

"And it also ain't gonna be easy since I don't even know what it was he was supposed to do for you."

"I might be able to tell you that later," O'Grady said, "but not right now."

Shoe seemed to be thinking it over for a few moments, and then he nodded to himself as if he had just made a decision.

"All right, then," Shoe said. "I'll do some nosin' and get back to you."

"Do you want some money now?" O'Grady asked.

"No," Shoe said, holding his hand up, "I'll keep a runnin' account and let you know what it comes to. I can trust you for the money, can't I?"

"You can trust me," O'Grady said, "about as much as I can trust you."

Shoe smiled and said, "Hell, *nobody* that trustworthy." He went out the door, cackling, and O'Grady had the feeling that he'd just made himself a good deal.

9

O'Grady made it down to the dining room just in time. He had just seated himself when Lisa appeared at the entranceway. The waiter greeted her and escorted her to O'Grady's table.

"Would you like to order lunch immediately?" Louis asked them.

"Well," O'Grady said, looking at Lisa, not at Louis, "to tell you the truth, it's not really food that I'm hungry for."

"Madam?" Louis said.

Lisa did the same thing; she answered Louis but kept her eyes on O'Grady.

"I feel the same way."

"As you wish," Louis said without batting an eye and walked away.

"Why don't we come down for a late lunch," O'Grady said to Lisa, "later."

"My feeling exactly," she replied.

O'Grady kept his hands on Lisa's head while she worked on him with her mouth. He was hard like a rock, and she was sliding her mouth over him, using her tongue as if she were a beautiful filly and he was a salt lick. She was wetting him thoroughly, moaning and cooing to him, enjoying every minute of it.

"Oh my, God," she said, "you're so beautiful . . . I can't believe how lovely you are . . ."

She cupped his genitals in her hands and proceeded to lick them, too, then worked her way back up the length of him until she could plant a wet kiss right on the spongy head of his cock. She swirled her tongue around him then, "umming" and "ooohing" some more, and then dropped her head down on him, taking him as far into her mouth as he would go. He was amazed at just how much of him she was able to take, and then when she started riding him with her mouth his amazement turned to wonder, his wonder to disbelief, and finally his disbelief to gratitude as he lifted his hips and literally exploded.

"You are the most beautiful man I've ever been with," she said, her head on his chest. He couldn't be sure, but he thought he felt tears running from her eyes and dropping hotly to his naked chest.

"Lisa," he said, running his hand lightly over her back, "I should be telling you that."

"Oh, no," she said, "you've been with a lot of beautiful women, Canyon. I know that. You can't tell them they're *all* the most beautiful. I've been with a lot of men, but never with one like you. Your body responds to everything I do to it, and you respond, and then you make my body respond . . . I've never known a man who could give as much pleasure as he got, and that's what I find truly amazing about you."

She raised her head and kissed him, a long, lingering kiss with a gentle probing of the tongue, and then she set her head back down on his chest again.

"Canyon?"

"Yes?"

"What are you *really* doing here in New Orleans?"

The question came so innocently that another man might have answered it in exactly the same manner. Canyon O'Grady was not another man, though; he was a man who had spent most of his life looking and listening for hidden meanings in the most innocent of words.

"We talked about that already," he said. "I'm a gambler."

"For a man who says he's a gambler," she said, "you have remarkably little interest in gambling."

"Is that so?"

She slid her hand down over his belly until she was holding his semierect penis in her hand, running her thumb over the head. "You're here for the gold, aren't you?" she asked.

"Gold?" he asked. "What gold is that, Lisa?"

She stopped then, stopped fondling him, stopped lying on him and, he thought, stopped pretending she was something that she was not. She got up on her knees and then settled back down on her haunches. He stared at her big breasts and fought the urge to reach out and cup them. He could see in here eyes that she had all but forgotten that they were both naked.

"We could help each other, you know," she said.

"To do what?"

"To find the gold," she said, "and then to spend it. Or we could just help each other find it, then split it and go our separate ways."

"That is presupposing that I do know what gold you're talking about."

"Yes," she said, "there is that, yes." She got up

off the bed, reached for her clothes, and started to dress.

"It's going to be very difficult for you to get near it," she said, "with the police following you everywhere you go." She looked at him then, and he looked at her. She was leaning down to slip her stockings on, and her breasts were hanging, swaying just a little bit. Her head was turned to the right, and she was actually looking up at him.

"You do know that the police are following you, don't you?"

"Oh, yes," she said, "I know it."

"Well, I don't know why they're following you, and I don't really care. Just as long as they don't get in our way."

"And just what is it that they might be getting in the way of, Lisa?"

She sat up then, put her hand on his leg, and then slid it up until it was on his thigh, just inches from his genitals.

"We can help each other, Canyon," she said. She slid her nails lightly over his inner thigh. "Think about it, won't you?"

"Sure, Lisa," he said, "I'll think about everything you've said here today."

She continued to dress then, and when she was finished she stood and looked down at him.

"Why don't we just skip lunch and have an early dinner later, instead?" she asked. "Say about five o'clock? That should be enough time for you to think things over, shouldn't it?"

"I could think about a lot of things between now and then," he said.

"Good," she said, smiling. "In the dining room then, at five."

"I'll be there," he promised.

"I know you will."

She leaned over and kissed him shortly, almost impersonally, and then left.

He slid his hands behind his head and stared up at the ceiling. Why, he wondered, had she chosen this particular time to reveal herself to him. Not that she had actually revealed anything about herself, except that she was in New Orleans looking for the gold, and that she knew—or thought she knew—that he was, too. He wondered if she knew—or thought she knew—why he was looking for the gold, because how could she know he was there looking for it if she didn't know he was working for the government.

It was funny. He had now spoken to two people about the gold, and they had both made an offer to help him find it and split it with him. LeClerc—he might have known where it was, but he didn't think Lisa did. If she did know where it was, she certainly wouldn't need his help, would she. Lisa Carlson struck him as the kind of woman who wouldn't split the gold, or anything of value, with anyone if she didn't have to.

No, Lisa didn't know where the gold was anymore than he did. There was no reason to go along with her then, save one, and that was to find out how she knew about the gold, and who, if anyone, she was working with.

Could she have been working with LeClerc, or was it more likely that she was responsible, at least in part, for LeClerc's death? And if that was the case, was she now seeking to win O'Grady's confidence so she could then set *him* up to be killed?

And did she really think she could win him over with her body . . . and her marvelous mouth . . . and her wonderfully talented hands?

O'Grady actually drifted off to sleep after that. He rose and dressed at three and came back downstairs. The policeman who had followed him that morning was nowhere to be seen, but his double was sitting on one of the sofas in the lobby. Of course this man was not actually the other man's double, but they were so similar that "double" seemed the right word. The man jerked upright when he saw O'Grady coming down the stairs and then seemed intent on looking anywhere but at the big agent.

O'Grady had an urge to go over to the man and inform him that he was just going to take a walk, but then he decided not to. There was no point in antagonizing Inspector Quitman by humiliating his men. Besides, the man would be humiliated enough later when O'Grady decided to lose him.

O'Grady stopped first at the desk and asked the clerk if there were any messages for him. "No, sir, no messages just now," the clerk said, "Uh, was the bellman satisfactory, sir?"

"So far," O'Grady said, "but I'll be able to tell you a lot better later on."

10

O'Grady walked around for a while, staying relatively close to the area of the hotel. The policeman who was following walked a respectable distance behind him. The big redheaded agent was thinking his situation over, factoring in everyone who had become involved during the past fifteen or twenty hours.

First there was Lisa, who had seemed innocent enough. Perhaps he'd been foolish to think that she had simply been attracted to him immediately—as he had been to her—and had wanted to go to bed with him for that reason. Well, why not? It had happened before. So this time was different. He was still very sure that she had enjoyed their time together as much as he had.

Then there was LeClerc, whose presence was very brief indeed, but he led to Inspector George Quitman. Quitman was suspicious of O'Grady—whether he suspected him of LeClerc's death, or was simply suspicious on general principle. Because of this, O'Grady had to factor his "tails" into every move he made.

And of course there was Shoe, whom he had drawn in himself. How little or much to tell Shoe was not a very important part of this. The little man knew the streets, but how much would he be able to do if he were kept completely in the dark? No, he was going to have to be told something. What, and how much, those were the questions.

And there were bound to be others, others who were undoubtedly already present, whom he didn't know about, yet. It was possible that Lisa had partners. It was also likely that there were those whose interests were outside his own and Lisa's—private interests and patriotic ones.

O'Grady didn't mind dealing with people who thought they were patriots. It was dealing with the zealots that he hated. You *never* knew what they would do, and neither did they. He'd learned the hard way in an almost impossible protection job with the president on the railroad, some time ago.

Finally he started back to the hotel. He crossed the street to the other side instead of simply turning in his tracks and panicking his tail. He hoped Inspector Quitman would appreciate how he was taking care of his men.

He was still several blocks from the hotel when he became aware of someone coming up behind him. He thought it might be the policeman approaching him for some reason, so he turned, and the movement saved his life, along with a shout from the policeman, who was still across the street.

The man behind him had a knife, and as O'Grady turned he was bringing it down. His intention had obviously been to bury the thing in the redhaired agent's back. O'Grady threw up his arm to block the blow. The knife actually tore the sleeve of his jacket as he parried the blow, but it just barely touched the skin.

The man's arm continued to swing downward as he fell off balance. O'Grady grabbed the man's arm by the wrist, turned it so that the elbow faced up, and then he brought his own elbow down hard. The result was that his attacker's arm bent the wrong way, and the man screamed in pain.

"Hey!" the policeman shouted again, running across the street.

O'Grady's attention was distracted for a moment by the policeman, and the man with the broken arm took advantage to push past him and run.

"Are you all right?" the policeman asked.

"Go after him," O'Grady said.

"Why?"

"You're a policeman!" O'Grady said. "He just tried to kill me."

Suddenly the young policeman seemed to realize he had made a mistake and had revealed himself.

"Hey," he said, backing away, "I'm not a policeman. I just saw what was happening and hollered out to you."

O'Grady looked at the man, whose eyes were pleading with him not to challenge his statement. The young man probably didn't want Inspector Quitman to know that he had given himself away.

"All right," O'Grady said, "forget it. Thanks for shouting."

"That's all right," the man said, "I'll just, uh, go now."

"Sure," O'Grady said, "go ahead."

He examined the sleeve of his jacket and then the flesh of his arm. There was a long scratch, but it was hardly bleeding. He had been very lucky. He bent over and retrieved the knife, a deadly, fine-honed blade only about five inches long. If it had not been so incredibly sharp, it might not have scratched him so cleanly. He was going to keep it, then decided there was no point. He started back to the hotel, pausing to drop the knife into a pile of trash in an alley.

There wasn't much more he could do at this point than wait for Shoe and keep an eye on Lisa Carlson. His best bet with her was just to play along until he found out what her real game was.

When he entered the hotel lobby Inspector George Quitman was sitting on one of the sofas, waiting for him. The policeman stood up as O'Grady approached. The other policeman, upon seeing his boss, simply moved over and leaned against a wall. He looked scared, afraid O'Grady might tell his boss what he'd done.

"Mr. O'Grady," Quitman said.

"Inspector," O'Grady replied. "Is there something I can help you with?"

"I was sort of hoping you could help me, yes," Quitman said.

"Can I buy you a cup of coffee inside?" O'Grady asked, indicating the dining room.

Quitman took a second to look at the dining room, then said, "No, I don't think so. Actually, I was just wondering if there was anything else you might have wanted to tell me?"

"About anything in particular?" O'Grady asked, hesitating for just a moment.

"Well, about the shooting last night would be nice," Quitman said. "Also, what you thought you were doing this morning."

"Well," O'Grady said, "there isn't anything about the shooting that I haven't told you, and I don't know what you mean about this morning."

"Those two fellas you sort of scared the hell out of at that little restaurant," Quitman explained. He folded his arms and said, "You know, after you sent your telegram?"

O'Grady wondered if Quitman had checked on the telegram itself.

"Oh, that," he said.

"Yes, that," Quitman said. "You told them you killed Anton LeClerc."

"No, no," O'Grady said, "I did no such thing."

"And you pointed out my man to them, knowing they'd run to him and tell him about it," Quitman said. "Now, were you just having fun with all of us, or what?"

"Well, see Inspector," O'Grady said, "those two fellas were all set to fight with me over a table. I just thought I'd avoid any kind of physical confrontations. I mean, if we had gotten into a fight and started damaging that restaurant, your man would have had to come running in to stop it, now wouldn't he?"

"Yes, I suppose he would."

"And I might have gotten hurt," O'Grady went on. "Or they might have gotten hurt, or your man might have gotten hurt, and I know somebody would have gotten embarrassed over it. The way I see it, I scared those two, but I kept anybody from getting hurt or being embarrassed. Do you see what I mean?"

Quitman stared at him for a few moments, then said, "Yes, I see what you mean, Mr. O'Grady."

"I'm glad," O'Grady said. "See, I don't want to have any misunderstandings between us, Inspector. I'm not looking to go up against you."

"Is that a fact?"

"It surely is."

"That's good, Mr. O'Grady," Quitman said, "because if you did go up against me, and you and me went round and round, you'd come out the loser. You know that, don't you?"

"I know that for a fact, Inspector Quitman," O'Grady said. "After all, this is your city. I'm just a visitor here."

"That's right," Quitman said, "you're just a visitor here." Quitman frowned then and asked, "What happened to your arm?"

"My arm's fine."

"The sleeve of your jacket . . ."

"Oh, that," O'Grady said, looking down at it. "I fell down."

"You fell down."

"That's right."

Quitman took a moment to look past O'Grady at his man, who was still lounging against the wall.

"Okay," Quitman said. "You fell down."

"That's right."

Quitman studied O'Grady for a few moments, then shrugged and said, "Are you sure there isn't something else you'd like to tell me about that shooting?"

It was O'Grady's turn to take a moment, as if he was thinking it over, then shook his head and said, "No, Inspector, I honestly can't think of a thing."

"Honestly," Quitman repeated.

O'Grady nodded and said, "Honestly."

"You and I are going to talk again, Mr. O'Grady," Quitman said, wagging his index finger at him. "Count on it."

"Oh, I know," O'Grady said. "I don't doubt that for a minute, Inspector."

"That's good." The inspector nodded, started to

walk away, then stopped and said, "One more thing, Mr. O'Grady."

"What's that, Inspector?"

"Stop having fun at the expenses of my men."

O'Grady smiled and said, "I'll do that, Inspector."

"You know," Quitman said, suddenly in no hurry to leave, "you signed the register stating you were from Washington."

"That's right," O'Grady said, "Washington, D.C."

"That's funny," Quitman said.

"Why funny?"

"Well, I've got a lot of friends in Washington, D.C. and I can't find out a thing about you. Don't you find that funny?"

"Well, Inspector," O'Grady said, "you know when you sign the register in a hotel you've got to put down something. I put Washington because that's where I'm originally from. In all honesty, though, I'm really not from anywhere in particular these days."

"Just traveling, huh?"

"That's right," O'Grady said, "traveling."

"Like most gamblers do."

"Occupational hazard, I guess," O'Grady said.

"I suppose so," Quitman said. "Well, I'm glad you cleared up that little mystery for me, O'Grady. It makes me feel a whole lot better."

"Glad I could help, Inspector."

"Yes," Quitman said, "I know you are."

As Quitman walked through the lobby toward the door his man studiously avoided looking over at him. At one point the inspector looked directly at the man, slowed down, shook his head, and then continued on out the door.

When his boss was gone the policeman looked over

at O'Grady anxiously. O'Grady put both hands out and made a settle-down gesture with them as though he was patting the air.

Before going up to his room O'Grady went to the desk to check for messages again. Where yesterday he might have gotten a message from Rufus Wheeler, today there were a lot more people who could be leaving him messages, most notably Shoe or Lisa.

"No, sir," the clerk said, "no messages."

"Thanks," O'Grady said. "Is Shoe around?"

"No, sir," the clerk said, "it was my understanding that Shoe was running an errand, uh, for you?"

"That's right," O'Grady said, "he is. I was just checking up on him."

"Oh, well, there's no reason for you to do that, sir," the clerk said. "I can assure you that Shoe is a very reliable person."

"I'm glad to hear that," O'Grady said, "I'm very glad to hear that."

O'Grady turned, took a quick glance at the policeman to make sure he was there, and then started up the stairs to his room. He still had about an hour before meeting Lisa—time enough for a bath and a change of clothes.

There was more than one man in the lobby of the hotel, watching Canyon O'Grady walk up the steps. One man in particular was sitting in an armchair by a huge potted plant, his legs crossed, seemingly perfectly relaxed. The only giveaway that he might not be as relaxed as he appeared was the constant rubbing of a scar through his left eyebrow with his right index finger. He was not a policeman although he noticed the policeman who was sitting across the lobby from him on the sofa.

The man watched O'Grady with interest, and although his instructions so far were not to approach the man or make a move on him in any way, he couldn't help but size the man up as a potential opponent, or rival. In either capacity, however, he felt that he would definitely be the superior of the two. Soon enough, he hoped, he would have the opportunity to find out for sure.

11

O'Grady bathed, washing the scratch on his arm with soap. He soaked in the tub and thought about the attempt on his life. There were a lot of possibilities.

Number one, he'd have to pay special attention to Lisa Carlson's reaction when he showed up in the dining room for dinner. It was possible that she or someone who worked with her was responsible for the attempt. He hoped to be able to read in her face whether she was involved or not.

Not knowing how many other factions were in New Orleans looking for the gold, he could not guess how many others might have been involved. Somebody obviously saw him as a threat, although the attempt on him was not a very professional one. Still, it might have been intended to look like a clumsy attempt at robbery that had ended tragically.

He stepped from the tub and donned fresh clothes. He was prepared to go right from the hotel bathhouse to the dining room without stopping in his room. He strapped on his gun and proceeded to do just that.

He was deliberately late because he wanted to be able to read her surprise, if there was any. She was already seated as he entered the dining room, and he paid special attention as she looked up and saw him.

She was beautiful, her dark hair swept up high on her head, her lovely pale shoulders exposed by the low-cut gown she wore. If she was expecting him to be dead there was not a flicker of surprise or disappointment on her face. If she had something to do with the attempt on his life, she was a superb actress.

He crossed the room and sat in the chair Louis held out for him.

"You're late," she said. "I hope you don't mind, but I ordered."

"I don't mind," he said.

She looked up at Louis and nodded, and he nodded in return.

"How was your day?" he asked.

"Uneventful," she said. "And yours?"

"Not so uneventful."

She frowned. "What happened?"

"Somebody tried to kill me today."

"Where?"

"On the street."

"How?"

"With a knife," he said. "From behind. It might have been a botched robbery."

She leaned forward, and the movement made her already impressive cleavage swell. "You don't believe that, do you?"

"Why not?"

"We're looking for the same thing, Canyon," she said. "I don't know how you found out about it, and I'm not going to tell you how I know about it, but we're obviously not the only ones who know. Somebody tried to eliminate you today."

"Maybe."

"No maybes about it," she said. "We've got to watch each other's backs from now on, that is, if we're going to work together."

He leaned forward and said, "We've worked together all right so far, I don't see any reason why we can't continue to."

"Does that mean that you agree?" she asked. "You accept my offer."

"Your offer of a partnership, right?"

"Yes, of course," she said. "A full partnership. A fifty-fifty split."

"Yes," he said, "I accept."

Louis came with the first course of their meal, which was followed by five or six more. After a while O'Grady lost count.

"Let me ask you something," he said during dessert.

"What?"

"Now that we're partners," he asked, "does that mean that we're going to split the cost of this meal right down the middle?"

"No," she said, "tonight is on me. Our partnership can start tomorrow."

"Or," he said, "it can start . . . oh, ten or fifteen minutes from now."

She stared back at him and said, "Oh, I think we can make it to your room from here in less time than that."

"Let's see . . ." he said.

As they stepped from the dining room O'Grady saw that a new policeman had taken up residence in the lobby. It was funny, but as much as they didn't want to be noticed, they all chose the same sofa to sit on.

Lisa noticed him as well. "They're remarkably easy to spot, aren't they?" she asked.

"Yes," he said, "they are."

"I wonder if they'll be as easy to lose?"

"I guess we'll know that when the time comes."

She linked her arm into his and they started up the steps.

She rode him hard in bed, so hard that the bed itself moved while they made love. Actually love had no part in what they were doing. They were enjoying each other, pure and simple, having sex. There was no other way to describe what they were doing.

She had both of her hands pressed onto his chest and was lifting her hips high and then coming down on him hard, swallowing him up inside of her. Every time he pierced her like that, she gasped and bit her lip, and he grunted aloud. O'Grady was never a man to hide what he was feeling in bed, and Lisa Carlson matched him exactly. The room filled with their cries and moans, and then his guttural roar and her high-pitched "Yessss!" as they crossed the border together . . .

"This is much better," she said later.

"What is?"

"This," she said, running her hands over him. "Being together without pretending. Now we can be natural with each other, and that makes the sex even better, don't you think?"

"Absolutely," he said. If she could lie, why couldn't he swear to it?

Still later, after she was sleeping with her head on his chest and his arm around her, he remembered what she had said in the lobby about the policemen being easy to spot. It occurred to O'Grady then that they might have been too easy to spot. Inspector Quitman did not seem at all a stupid or foolish man, so putting such obvious tails on O'Grady could not be the result of foolishness or stupidity. That meant the act was shrewd.

There was a second tail, one that O'Grady had not yet spotted. Quitman was assigning young, inexperienced officers as his primary tail so that O'Grady would spot them. Then, when O'Grady made a move to lose them, the more experienced secondary tail would take over.

O'Grady suddenly had renewed respect for the inspector. It never occurred to him that he might be giving the man too much credit. He was now sure that he was being followed by at least two policemen at a time. In the morning he was going to have to work very hard at identifying that secondary tail without seeming to have done so.

He also decided that he would not tell Lisa what he had just figured out. Having a policeman following them that she did not know about might actually come in handy later on.

Down in the lobby the man with the scar decided that O'Grady and Lisa Carlson were not coming back downstairs tonight. He had a room in the smaller hotel down the street, and he rose now, preparing to leave and turn in for the night. He started for the door, then stopped, turned, and looked at the policeman who was still sitting on the sofa. An idea crossed his mind, a delicious idea that would cause a stir and possibly take O'Grady out of play without his ever having braced the man physically. Now wouldn't doing it that way truly prove his superiority over the redhaired man?

He walked over to the policeman on the sofa and sat down next to him. There was room for an extremely thin person to sit between them, if one so desired.

"Excuse me," he said to the policeman.

"Hmm? Yes?"

"Excuse me," the man with the scar said again. He wanted the man to look at him, which he did finally.

"Would you mind coming outside with me?" he asked the policeman.

"I beg your pardon?"

"Outside," the man said. "I have something to show you."

The policeman was one of Inspector Quitman's more inexperienced men. He looked around the lobby for the more experienced member of the team, but that man had gone home already. During the night Quitman had decided to leave only the first man on duty and remove the second man until morning. That left this particular policeman on his own for the moment.

"I'm sorry," the policeman said, nervously, "Uh, I can't leave here—"

"You are a policeman, aren't you?" the man with the scar asked.

"Uh, what? I'm sorry, no, you must have me confused . . ." the younger man stammered, beginning to deny it without much conviction.

"Steady," the man with the scar said. "Look under my arm, right here."

The policeman did so and saw that the scar-faced

man whom he had not even noticed sitting across the lobby from him, was now pointing a gun at him from beneath his left arm. The man wagged the gun a little to make sure that the policeman saw it.

"Outside," the man said to him, "now."

"Okay," the policeman said, "okay . . ."

12

The pounding on his door woke O'Grady and Lisa the next morning.

"What is it?" she asked, sleepily.

"I don't know."

He got out of bed, hurriedly put his pants on, and opened the door just as someone started at it again. He was surprised to see Inspector Quitman standing in the hallway, his hand raised for more pounding.

"Get dressed," Quitman said, "you're coming with me."

"What?" O'Grady asked. "Where? What for?"

"Never mind," Quitman said. "Just get dressed and come on."

"Inspector," O'Grady said, "I have a guest—"

"Send the bitch back to her own room and come on!" Quitman said. This was the closest O'Grady had seen the man to losing control.

"Inspector," O'Grady said, playing at being outraged, "I'm not going anywhere until you tell me what the hell is going on."

"I've got a dead police officer on my hands, that's what it's about."

"So?" O'Grady asked. "What does that have to do with me?"

"He was assigned to watch you, that's what it has to do with you," Quitman said. "Now, are you coming or do I have to have a couple of men drag you down the stairs and through the lobby in chains?"

"I'm coming, Inspector, I'm coming," O'Grady said. "Just let me get dressed."

"I'll be waiting right here," Quitman said, folding his arms.

O'Grady closed the door and walked back to the bed to retrieve his clothes.

"What's going on?" Lisa said. "Did he say something about a dead policeman?"

"That's what he said."

"And he thinks you had something to do with it?"

"I don't know what he things," O'Grady said, "but I'll bet I'm going to find out soon enough."

"He can't think that though," she said. "You were here with me all last night."

He looked at her and said, "Hold that thought. I might need you to say just that, in a little while."

During the ride to headquarters Inspector Quitman maintained a strained silence. O'Grady noticed that the other two policemen on the wagon kept casting angry glances his way. O'Grady figured he was pretty lucky to have spent the night with Lisa last night. It might just keep him out of jail. When they reached police headquarters Quitman said, "Go with these two officers. I'll be along shortly."

O'Grady nodded and obeyed. He figured the best way to get through this fast was to cooperate.

He was put in the same room in which Quitman had questioned him the first time. After about fifteen minutes the inspector entered and dismissed the other two men. "I had an officer in the lobby," Quitman said.

"He was supposed to stay there all night until relieved. This morning when his relief showed up, he wasn't there. The relief man got worried and started looking around."

"And?" O'Grady prompted.

"He found him behind the hotel, thrown in with the trash. He'd been strangled."

"So you're pulling me in?" O'Grady said. "What would I have to gain by killing one of your men?"

"He was assigned to follow you," Quitman said. "Maybe you had someplace you wanted to go without being followed."

"So I killed him?" O'Grady said. "Come on, Quitman, your men wouldn't be that hard to lose, if that's what I wanted to do. Why should I kill one of them and bring you down on me like this? It doesn't make sense." He decided not to tell the inspector that he had figured out that he was being followed by two policemen, a primary and secondary tail. That knowledge was an ace in the hole he wanted to hold on to. "Does it?"

"No," Quitman said, "it doesn't make sense, O'Grady, but then I don't know you well enough to know whether or not you only do things that make sense."

"Don't you?" O'Grady asked.

Quitman stared back at him.

"Didn't anyone in the lobby see anything?" O'Grady asked. "I mean, if he was supposed to be in the lobby what was he doing behind the hotel?"

"I don't know."

"No one saw anything?"

"No."

88

"Someone must have made him leave the lobby," O'Grady said. "Are you sure no one saw—"

"We checked, damn it!" Quitman said. "No one saw a thing. It could have happened late, when there was no one in the lobby but the desk man."

That meant that the secondary tail was pulled off during the night. Something else that was useful for O'Grady to know. "Look, Inspector," O'Grady said, "I'm sorry your man was killed, I really am, but I didn't do it."

"He was strangled by someone with very strong hands," Quitman said. "A big, strong man . . . like you."

"There are a lot of big, strong men in New Orleans, Inspector."

"Maybe," Quitman said, "but you're the one he was assigned to."

"Granted," O'Grady said, "but I have a witness. The lady I was with can tell you that I was with her all night long."

"That's good, O'Grady," Quitman said. "It's good that you've got someone who will do that for you. Just give me her name and I'll check it out."

O'Grady told Quitman Lisa's full name, and that she was also a guest in the hotel.

"I'll be talking to her," Quitman said.

"Can I leave?"

"Yes," Quitman said, "you're free to go . . . for now, but don't even think about leaving New Orleans. Do you understand?"

"I understand perfectly, Inspector," O'Grady assured him. He started for the door, then turned again before leaving and said, "I'm truly sorry about your man, Inspector."

"He was young . . ." Quitman said. He seemed to want to say more, but finally he waved O'Grady away, and the agent left.

On the way back to the St. Charles in a coach O'Grady thought about the murder of the policeman. Was it an unconnected fact that the man was assigned to him? If it was, then it was coincidence, and O'Grady didn't like coincidences. It meant someone had killed that policeman as a message. . . . A message to Canyon O'Grady? Or to someone else?

And what was the message? If we'll kill a policeman we won't hesitate to kill you? Were they trying to warn him, or to scare him away?

Was it Lisa? Would she work at getting him to be partners with her, and then try to scare him off? That made about as much sense as figuring her to be behind the attempt on his own life yesterday.

O'Grady wondered if the officer who saw the attempt the day before would decide to tell Quitman about it. If he did, the inspector was going to be very interested to know why a man who was supposedly just visiting New Orleans would not report an attempt on his life.

13

"You're an idiot!" Lisa Carlson said.

The man with the scar frowned at her. His name was Clapton, and he was partners with Lisa Carlson. Lisa had come to him with news of a cache of gold hidden in New Orleans, a city he knew quite well.

"Take it easy, Lisa," he said, warningly. "Don't forget that we're partners in this. Don't try talking to me like an employee."

"I'm talking to you like what you are," Lisa said, "an idiot."

"Damn it, woman—"

"Well then tell me what the hell you were thinking when you killed that policeman?" she demanded.

Clapton sat back on his bed, folded his hands across his lean belly, and smiled benignly. "Who said I killed anyone?"

"Come on, Clap," she said. "He was strangled. You love that."

He looked down at his hands, which were large and strong for such a slender man. In truth, Ben Clapton's build belied the strength he truly possessed. "What if I say I didn't do it?"

"I'd say you were a liar."

"I'm warning you, Lisa—"

"I have to get back before he gets back," she said. "I just wanted to see you and satisfy myself that you did it."

"I haven't said—"

"You don't have to," she said. "I can see it in your face."

As she headed for the door he called out, "I still don't see why we need him."

"You don't have to," she said. "I do."

She went out, slamming the door behind her. On the street she broke into a run, wanting to get back to the room before O'Grady.

As O'Grady entered the hotel he stopped at the desk to ask about messages.

"No, sir, no messages," the man said. "You're up early this morning."

"Not by choice," O'Grady said.

"I thought perhaps you were meeting Miss Carlson," the man said.

O'Grady stopped several steps away from the desk, turned, and came back. "What was that?"

"I'm sorry, sir," the man said. "It's none of my business. I just thought perhaps that you and she—"

"Was Miss Carlson downstairs already this morning?" O'Grady asked.

"Why, yes sir."

"When?"

"A short while ago," the man said. "She went out and returned shortly after. In fact, she came in just a few minutes ahead of you, sir."

"I see," O'Grady said.

"If I've offended you, sir—"

"No, you haven't," O'Grady said. "Don't worry about it, all right? And don't mention it to anyone."

"I won't," the clerk said fervently. His friends and family were right, he thought. He did talk too much.

"But why would they suspect you?" Lisa asked.

When O'Grady had returned to his room she was in bed, supposedly still asleep. She "awoke" when he walked in and asked him what had happened. Her question came after he explained it all to her.

"He was assigned to follow me," he said. "Lisa, maybe you should get yourself a new partner. I've got a hell of a lot more attention than I want."

"No, it's all right," she said. She drew her knees up beneath the sheet and wrapped her arms around them. "If it's all right, I'll stick with my first choice."

"It's all right with me," he said. "I was just thinking of you."

"I have to have a bath," she said, "and get dressed."

She got out of bed, came to him, and pressed herself to him, kissing him. He slid his hands down her back to her haunches and cupped them.

"Too bad they had to wake us up like that," she whispered. "I had an entirely different idea of a way to wake you."

With his hands on her buttocks he lifted her up and carried her to the bed. He dropped her on it, and she stared up at him, her arms thrown over her head.

"It's not too late," he said.

He leaned over and buried his face between her breasts. . . .

After Lisa left to take her bath and get dressed O'Grady removed yesterday's clothes and washed himself using the basin and pitcher on the dresser. Bare-chested, he walked to the window and stared out at the street below.

In the face of the attention he was getting from the police—with more to come—why would Lisa still want him for a partner? The answer to that seemed very simple to him. It was not a partner she was looking for, but a scapegoat. For what, this murder?

Two people were dead already, LeClerc and the policeman, and both deaths had to have something to do with the gold. But he still had no idea where to start even looking.

What the hell had happened to Shoe? Would he turn up dead, too? He got dressed, strapped on his gun, and went downstairs. He was interested to see who would be in the lobby, waiting to follow him today. Also, he wanted to try to spot that secondary tail.

The lobby was busy, and the sofa where all of the policemen had chosen to sit yesterday was empty today. He descended the steps very slowly, so that he had time to take in the entire lobby. It was too crowded at the moment to pick out a tail. He decided that a leisurely breakfast was in order and went into the dining room. He allowed Louis to show him to a table.

"Will you be eating alone this morning, Mr. O'Grady?" Louis asked.

"Yes, Louis, I expect I will be," he said.

"Very good, sir."

He ordered but then stopped Louis before he would walk away. "Louis, did you hear about what happened today?"

"The murder, sir? Of the policeman?"

"That's right."

"Oh yes, sir. All of the kitchen staff has heard of it

because he was found in our trash. I'm sure the entire hotel staff had heard of it by now. A shocking thing."

"Yes, it is," O'Grady said and allowed the waiter to go and put his order in.

Louis returned with a pot of coffee and one cup. "Louis, do you know Shoe?" O'Grady asked while the man poured.

"Yes, sir," the waiter said. "I expect everyone in the hotel knows Shoe."

"Has he been around this morning?"

"Not that I know of, sir."

"I see."

"Excuse me, sir?"

"Yes?"

"Excuse me for asking, but do you have Shoe, uh, doing a job of work for you?"

"As a matter of fact, I do, Louis. Why?"

"Well . . . you should know that, in certain circles, Shoe is considered, er, disreputable."

"It just so happens that for this particular job of work, Louis," O'Grady said, "I was looking for someone a bit disreputable."

"Well then, sir," Louis said, "I would say that you chose quite well."

"I'm glad to hear that, Louis," O'Grady said. "Tell me, in what circles is Shoe considered disreputable?"

Louis gave him a surprised look and then said, "Why, in reputable circles, sir."

"Of course," O'Grady said. "Silly of me."

"Breakfast will be here shortly, sir."

"Thank you, Louis."

14

Shoe finally put in an appearance while O'Grady was having breakfast, the little man appeared at the entrance to the dining room. He must have been standing there for a few moments before O'Grady looked up and saw him. The agent beckoned him to enter, but Shoe shook his head and signaled with his hand and head that O'Grady should meet him outside. O'Grady nodded, and Shoe disappeared.

O'Grady called Louis over and settled up for his breakfast, then left the dining room, walked through the lobby, and left the hotel.

Outside Shoe was waiting, appearing nervous.

"Where have you been?" O'Grady asked.

"Doing what you asked me to do," Shoe said, looking around.

"Well, what have you got?"

"We've got to go someplace and talk," Shoe said. "I don't want to end up dead."

"If you stay with me you won't," O'Grady said. "The police have someone following me."

Shoe looked at O'Grady and said, "You think I trust the police anymore than I trust anyone else? No, if you're being followed we got to lose them."

"That might be hard to do," O'Grady said.

"Why?"

"Well, yesterday I knew who was following me. Today I don't."

"Don't matter," Shoe said. "We'll have to pick him out. Come on, cross over." They crossed the street together and then waited to see who came out of the hotel.

"What's going on, Shoe?" O'Grady asked. "Did you find somebody who knew LeClerc."

"I found a lot of people who knew him," Shoe said, "but I only found one who claimed to be his partner."

"His partner?"

"That's right," Shoe said, "and that partner don't want to end up dead, like LeClerc."

"Is he willing to meet me?"

Shoe held up his hand for O'Grady to wait. The front door of the hotel opened, and a man stepped out. He looked both ways, then made a show of lighting a cigarette while glancing across the street.

"Okay, let's go," Shoe said. "That's him."

"Just like that? You figure that's my tail?"

"Figure, nothin'," Shoe said. "I know that man. His name's Jerry Kennealy."

"He's a policeman?"

"One of the best," Shoe said. "He wouldn't be easy to lose, so we ain't gonna try."

"So what do we do?"

"We'll just let him follow us," Shoe said. "Him I do trust."

They started down the street, and Kennealy kept pace with them from across the street.

"He knows I saw him, too," Shoe said, "and he

knows me." Shoe actually looked calmer. "We're okay with him coverin' our backs."

"How can you be so sure of him?"

"He's been a lawman of one kind or another for twenty-five years," Shoe said. "It's in his blood. There ain't nothin' else he *can* do, and he wouldn't turn crooked for all the money in the world."

"Must be nice to be that sure of somebody."

"I'm more sure of him than I am of you," Shoe said. "You must be pretty important if they put Kennealy on you. You want to tell me what's got everybody so spooked?"

"I don't know if I do or not," O'Grady said. "How do I know I can trust you?"

Shoe laughed and said, "You can't. I been hustlin' for a livin' too long to be trusted—unless I'm your partner, that is."

"Why is that?"

"Because I ain't never turned on a partner in my life," Shoe said, "and I'm too old to start now, just like Kennealy, back there. Too old to change."

They walked in silence for a while. O'Grady had no idea if they were just walking, or if they were actually going somewhere.

"All right," he said.

"All right, what?"

"All right, I'll take you on as a partner."

"An equal partner?"

"No," O'Grady said, "not an equal partner." In the big picture O'Grady's partner was the United States Government, although in that case it was he who was not an equal partner. "But I'll make sure that if I find what I'm looking for you'll make out better than you ever had in the past."

"That's pretty vague," Shoe said.

"It's the best I can do," O'Grady said. "Take it or leave it."

Now it was Shoe's turn to walk in silence and think things over. O'Grady controlled his urge to turn around to see if Kennealy was still with them.

"Well," Shoe said finally, "whatever this is it must be something big. Two people are dead, including a policeman, Kennealy's on it, and LeClerc's partner is as nervous as a cat."

"What do you know about the policeman who was killed?" O'Grady asked.

"Just that he was," Shoe said with a shrug. "You probably know more about that than I do."

"I know what you know," O'Grady said, "that he was killed, strangled."

Shoe looked at him and said, "See? I didn't know he was strangled. How?"

"Somebody strong did it with his hands."

Shoe rubbed his jaw.

"What do you know now?" O'Grady asked.

"Not much, but I can nose around," he said. "Most of the bad men I know who like to strangle people always use something other than their hands—a belt, a rope, a piece of wire. Using your hands, that's real personal. That's somebody who likes it."

"We can leave that to the police, Shoe," O'Grady said. "There's something else I'm after."

"And you're gonna tell me what that is, right?" Shoe asked.

O'Grady sighed and said, "I guess I am. . . ."

About twenty yards back, across the street, Police Officer Jerry Kennealy was wondering what Shoe and O'Grady were doing together. Shoe he knew; the little man had been hustling a living on the streets of New Orleans for a long time. O'Grady, that was a different story. Kennealy knew only what Inspector Quitman had told him, that O'Grady was connected with the killings of Anton LeClerc and the policeman, Officer Bishop.

Kennealy was a rugged-looking man with a weathered face. Although now in his early fifties he had the physique of a man ten years younger. He had been concerned with upholding the law in New Orleans since the city was actually three separate municipalities rather than one. It was only in 1852 that the city was united under one mayor and city council. It was then that the police department he was now a member of was first formed.

New Orleans had been a hotbed of violence, vice, and corruption for a long time, and the police department was a haphazard one, at best, with officers reporting for duty when they pleased. Kennealy knew only one man in the department, if it could be called that, whom he trusted—Inspector Quitman. If the department only had more men like Quitman running it . . .

Quitman thought O'Grady was holding something back, something that would explain the murders of the two men. Now that Kennealy saw O'Grady with Shoe, he tended to agree. Shoe would not be involved unless there was something big in it for him.

Kennealy knew he was going to need help though,

if he was going to keep an eye on them, because Shoe knew who he was. He was sure that the little man had already identified him to O'Grady. He'd have a talk with Shoe later on, but he was going to have to get another officer to help follow these two, someone who would do what he was told and would not muck everything up. For the life of him though, he couldn't think of one man.

Ben Clapton had seen O'Grady leave the hotel, but as he rose to follow him he saw another man do the same. Clapton decided to hold back a moment and allow the other man to leave first. He gave him a few seconds head start, then left the hotel. He saw O'Grady and a smaller man walking across the street, and the other man was following them on this side. Clapton stroked the scar on his eyebrow for a moment, then decided that instead of following he'd go back inside, sit, and wait. O'Grady would have to return to the hotel eventually. Also, following a man who was following a man tended to lead to something that looked like a procession. Clapton did not need to be spotted, not this time.

If Ben Clapton had not been completely captivated by Lisa Carlson—it would never occur to him to use the word *love*—he would have done away with Canyon O'Grady long ago. Because it was Lisa who had come to him with the information about the gold—information she had obtained while sharing the bed of a southern gentleman who fancied himself a big man—Clapton was allowing her to call the shots. He didn't agree with the way she was going about things, but he was willing to let her have her way for a while longer. But just a little while longer.

15

At a certain point during their walk O'Grady realized that Shoe had walked them in a circle, and they were actually on their way back to the St. Charles Hotel.

"Gold," Shoe said, shaking his head.

"That's right."

"That word does strange things to people," Shoe said. "I've seen it before."

"So have I."

"So do you think the murder of the policeman also has something to do with the gold?"

"It would be too much of a coincidence to be otherwise," O'Grady said.

"Not in this town," Shoe said. "People are gettin' killed all the time. Haven't you been readin' *The Delta, The True Delta,* and some of the other papers?"

"I haven't read any papers since I've been here," O'Grady said.

"Well, take my word for it, somebody's gettin' killed every day."

"That may be," O'Grady said, "but not somebody who was assigned to follow me. No, even if what you say is true, it would still be too much of a coincidence."

They walked in silence awhile, and then Shoe asked, "What should I tell Kennealy?"

"What makes you think you'll have to tell him anything?"

"Trust me on this," Shoe said. "After you and I split up, he'll stop me to have a chat. What was I doin' with you, how much you're payin' me, and all that."

"I have a feeling you'll know how to handle him," O'Grady said.

"Yeah, well, I been doin' it for a while," Shoe said.

"Are you and he friends?"

"I wouldn't say that," Shoe said, "but we been goin' back and forth for a few years."

"Tell me about the police department here."

"It ain't much of a department," Shoe said. "If it wasn't for Kennealy and Quitman, I wouldn't think nothin' of it. This city is wide open, Mr. O'Grady, and there ain't much that anybody's tryin' to do about it right now."

"So why stay?" O'Grady asked.

"Are you askin' me personal?"

"Yes."

Shoe looked at O'Grady and said, "Because this city is wide open, Mr. O'Grady."

O'Grady nodded and said, "Call me Canyon."

"Okay, Canyon."

"Tell me about the partner."

"Well, he *claims* to be LeClerc's partner."

"Does that mean that he knew what LeClerc knew?" O'Grady asked.

"I don't know," Shoe said. "I don't know what he knows, because I don't know what LeClerc knew. Do you?"

"LeClerc claimed that he knew enough to lead me to the gold."

"Well, you're gonna have to ask his partner if he knows that."

"Who is he?"

"If I tell you his name, it's not gonna mean anythin' to you."

"When can I meet with him then?"

"Tonight."

"Where?" O'Grady asked. "Not by the cathedral. I've done that already."

"No," Shoe said. "He's got someplace else in mind."

"Where?"

"A whorehouse, on Basin Street."

"You'll take me there?"

"Sure," Shoe said. "I have to. He won't talk to you if he doesn't see me. See, he's not convinced that you didn't kill LeClerc yourself."

"Why would I do that?"

Shoe shrugged. "He figures you might have found out what you wanted to from LeClerc and then killed him."

"Then why would I be looking for someone else to help me?"

Shoe shrugged again. "This fella we're gonna see is not the smartest guy in the world, Canyon," he said.

"All right, then," O'Grady said. "What time?"

"I'll come for you at nine," Shoe said. "There's just one thing you gotta do."

"What's that?"

"Lose Kennealy."

O'Grady laughed.

"If he's as good as you say he is, how am I going to lose him when we're in his arena and not mine?"

"I'll tell you," Shoe said. "Listen close . . ."

When they reached the hotel Shoe simply sheared off and kept walking while O'Grady entered the hotel. Kennealy hesitated only a second, then decided he'd better have that talk with Shoe right away rather than wait. Besides, he doubted that O'Grady would be going out again so soon. The policeman quickened his pace until he had caught up to Shoe. "Hey, Shoe."

"Hello, Kennealy," Shoe said, without stopping.

Kennealy, not a tall man, nevertheless towered over the diminutive Shoe. He put his hand on the smaller man's shoulder to stop him. "I've got a few questions," Kennealy said.

"How did I guess?" Shoe asked.

"What do you know about the man you were just talking to?"

"Would it work if I was to ask 'what man?' " Shoe asked.

"No."

"I didn't think so," Shoe said. "All I know is he's worried that the police—you fellas—might blame him for Anton LeClerc's murder."

"So he's asked you for help?"

Shoe looked at Kennealy and asked, "Is that so unbelievable?"

"What are you doing, Shoe, working as a private detective now?"

"You know," Shoe said, "I hadn't thought about that. I mean, he asked the desk clerk who knew the streets, and he gave him my name. When I talked to him he asked me to help him."

"How?"

"By asking questions."

"That's all?"

"What else could I do, Kennealy?" Shoe asked with a shrug. "After all, I'm not a detective, right?"

"I'm going to have my eye on you from now on, Shoe," Kennealy said. "That man O'Grady's involved in something, and now so are you, and I'm going to find out what it is."

"How are you gonna keep an eye on me," Shoe asked, "when you're supposed to be keepin' an eye on *him*?"

Kennealy smiled and said, "I've got two eyes, Shoe." With that he turned and headed back to the hotel.

Shoe watched him for about half a block, then turned and started on his way again.

Kennealy got back to the hotel in time to meet his relief man. The man told him he had arrived just in time to see O'Grady go up to his room.

"Where were *you*?" the man asked him.

"I was working," Kennealy said. "Look, I'll be back in a couple of hours."

"You ain't due back until tomorrow," the man said.

"I know," Kennealy answered. "I'm taking this thing on full time."

The other man looked at Kennealy as if he was crazy—everybody in the department knew Jerry Kennealy was crazy. "Hell," the man said with a shrug, "you can have it."

Ben Clapton watched the two policemen talk, and then the older one left. He didn't like the look of the older one. He appeared to be a man who had been around, a man who could take care of himself. He might be a man who could get in the way. Clapton looked down at his powerful hands and flexed his fingers.

16

There was a knock on O'Grady's door, insistent but not a man's knock. He opened the door and admitted Lisa Carlson.

"It's time to get to work," she said.

"Fine."

"What do you know?"

"Nothing," he said. "What do you know?"

She frowned at him. "Being partners means sharing what we know . . . you know?"

"I know," he said, "but I don't know anything."

"You must."

"Why?"

She hesitated a moment, then said, "Because *I* don't know anything."

"If I don't, you don't, right?"

"Canyon—"

"All right," O'Grady said. "Here's what I know. Somewhere in New Orleans is a cache of gold, enough to possibly finance a war or the start of a war."

"War?"

"Between the North and the South," he said. "Over slavery."

"Why would anyone fight over that?" she asked.

It looked as if she truly did not understand the concept.

"Some people are for, and some are against," he said. "Sometimes what they're for or against doesn't even matter, just being for or against is enough for some people to start a war over."

"That's crazy," she said. "I can see fighting over something, something that you can touch, but to fight over something you can't feel?"

"Ideals," O'Grady said. "People fight over ideals, and a lot of them feel their ideals."

"I'm talking about feeling something physically," she said, putting her hand on his arm and squeezing to illustrate her point. "I don't know anything about ideals."

"The question is," he said, "do you know anything about the gold?"

She took her hand away, folded her arms beneath her breasts, and walked around the room a bit.

"All right," she said, "there's one thing I know for sure."

"And that is?"

"The gold isn't buried," she said. "It's hidden, but it isn't buried."

"But there *is* gold," he said.

"Oh," she said, "there is gold. I know that, too."

"How do you know?" He knew that by asking he was maybe opening a can of worms. Once she told him how she knew, she was going to want to know how he knew.

"Let's just say I shared a pillow with a man who

knew," she said. "He liked to talk . . . you know, after . . . and he liked to sound important."

"How do you know he wasn't just trying to sound important?" O'Grady asked.

She gave him a bold stare and said, "I can tell when men are lying to me, Canyon."

"Can you?"

"Oh, yes," she said, "it's something I learned at a very early age. You see I developed into a woman very early. I was still a child in my mind, but at an early age I had the body of a woman, and men—grown men—used to lie to me all the time, so I'd let them . . . do things."

Suddenly he found himself feeling sorry for the little girl she was at one time.

"It took me a few years to catch on, but finally I did," she said. "I could tell when they were lying, I knew what they wanted, and I started to make them pay for it." She looked at him sharply then and added, "That did not make me a whore. What it did was put me in control."

"I understand."

"Do you?" she asked. "I don't know if a man could ever understand."

"Then I sympathize," he said.

She graced him with a smile and said, "All right, that I'll accept, but I'll also accept something else."

"What?"

"Tell me how you know about the gold."

"I need another man," Kennealy said to Quitman, "one I can trust."

"Take your pick," Quitman said.

"No," Kennealy said, "not from inside. I don't trust any of these men."

"You trust me, don't you?" Quitman asked.

"Of course I do."

"Then I'll be your second man."

"You can't," Kennealy said. "Both O'Grady and Shoe know you already."

"O'Grady knows you."

"He saw me today," Kennealy said. "He won't see me again. It's different with Shoe. I need someone that crafty little man doesn't know."

Quitman frowned across his desk at Kennealy. Jerry Kennealy didn't belong here. He thought so ever since he had met the man. Kennealy belonged in some big, well-organized city police department. Certainly not in wide open New Orleans where the law was a joke. "Do you have someone in mind?" Quitman asked.

"I do," Kennealy said, "and he's not a policeman."

"Will he do it?"

"Oh, he'll do it," Kennealy said, smiling.

Quitman frowned again. The smile had nothing whatsoever to do with humor. "Okay," Quitman said, "get him."

"I make it my business to hear things like that," O'Grady said.

"I thought being a gambler was your business." she asked.

O'Grady smiled. "My business is making money for myself," O'Grady said, "any way that I can. For that reason I keep my ear to the ground. I listen, I learn, and then I act."

"Like with this gold?" she asked. "But where did you hear about it?"

"In Washington."

"The Capitol?" she asked, her eyes widening.

"Yes."

"Then what you said about a war . . ."

"It's what I heard," O'Grady said.

"But . . . you'd take the gold anyway?"

"Wouldn't you?"

"Of course," she said, "but I thought—"

"What? That I had ideals?" He shook his head. "I know what they are, Lisa. That doesn't mean that I have them. I'm like you. I believe in what I can touch."

She opened her mouth to say something but he reached out, grabbed her, pulled her to him, and kissed her. He slid his hands down to cup her buttocks, thrusting his tongue into her mouth. He kissed her hard and long, and when he stopped she was breathless, staring at him.

"What I can feel," he said, opening the buttons at the back of her dress, "like this." He slid his hands inside so that his palms were on her hot flesh. She moaned and pushed her hand between them down to his crotch.

"Yes . . ." she said as he peeled her dress from her.

When she was naked he laid her down on the bed and started caressing her body with his hands and his mouth. He kissed her neck, her breasts, and sucked her nipples while his hands moved over her. When the fingers of his right hand pierced her she gasped and a tremor ran through her. She grabbed at his shirt then, tearing the buttons off as she fought to get it off him.

At least this way, he thought, she wasn't asking any questions.

17

O'Grady stared at the ceiling, listening to Lisa's breathing as she slept next to him. There was no way she could be faking the pleasure she experienced when they were in bed together. He didn't think she'd ever hesitate to use sex to get what she wanted—hell, that was how she found out about the gold—but he didn't think she was using it on him. Maybe she thought she was using it on him, but when they were in bed together he was sure that she was not faking. Still, that didn't mean that she wouldn't kill him if she thought it meant that she'd get the gold.

"What are you thinking?" she asked.

"I thought you were asleep," he said.

"I was," she replied, rolling onto her back, "but you were thinking so loud that it woke me up. What were you thinking about?"

"You."

"What about me?"

He sat up and propped his back against the bedpost, looking down at her. She was lying on her back, the sheet covering her breasts.

"Did you know a man named Anton LeClerc?"

She thought a moment and said, "LeClerc . . . no, I don't think I did. Did? Does that mean he's dead?"

"Yes," he said. "He was killed two nights ago."

"Killed? How?"

"He was shot to death. The police think I had something to do with it."

"Did you?"

"I was there," he said, "but they don't know why I was there."

"Why were you there?"

"He was going to tell me something about the gold."

"Something?"

"I think he knew where it was." O'Grady said, "He just needed help going to get it."

She sat up now, holding her sheet so that it continued to cover her. He didn't think she was doing this out of any sense of modesty. It *was* a little chilly in the room.

"Did he say anything about the gold?"

"He didn't have time," O'Grady said. "Somebody shot him and then took a couple of shots at me."

"Did you see who it was?"

"No," he said. "I chased them, but I never got a good look." He turned to her and asked, "Do you know anything about it?"

"No," she said—too quickly, he thought. "No, I told you, I don't know any LeClerc."

"There was a policeman killed last night," O'Grady said.

"I heard about that."

"Did you have anything to do with that?"

She was apparently taken aback by the question. "What do you think I am, Canyon?" she asked. "Why are you asking me if I had anything to do with two men being killed?"

"Since we're not pretending with each other, Lisa," he said, "I'll answer your question. I think you're a woman who would do whatever she had to do to get her hands on that gold. If that means killing a man like LeClerc, or a policeman . . . or *me*, I think you'd do it."

She stared at him in silence, then looked straight ahead at the wall, biting her bottom lip. "All right," she said, "I'm a hard bitch, Canyon. I always have been. Yes, I guess I'd kill to get what I wanted if I wanted it badly enough, but I didn't have anything to do with killing those men." She looked at him and said, "That you can believe."

He did believe it. She *had* qualified her statement, though. The way she spoke said that she had nothing to do with the killings personally. It didn't say that she didn't know anything about them. Of course he couldn't hold that against her. After all, he wasn't being totally honest with her, either.

Jerry Kennealy entered the gunsmith shop and closed the door behind him. It was musty inside, as if the door and the window were never open. That didn't surprise him. The man who owned the shop had been trying to keep the outside outside for a long time. "Abel?" he called.

There was a back room behind the counter, the doorway hidden by a curtain. The curtain parted, and Abel Triplett stepped through.

"Jerry," he said. Abel Triplett was a tall, slender man of fifty-five who had been a gunsmith for the past ten years but still moved like what he was—a tracker, hunter and, when called for, killer. "What brings you here?"

"You do, old friend."

Triplett smiled, and it was a sad smile. "Are you going to offer once again to take me away from all of this?" Triplett asked, spreading his hands to indicate his world.

"Not permanently, Abel," Kennealy said, "just for a little while."

"You need help?"

"I do."

"And I owe you." It was a statement, not a fact.

"I'm not calling in any markers, Abel," Kennealy said. "I'm just asking you for your help. Give it freely, or don't give it freely."

Triplett closed his eyes and looked at something only he could see. When he opened them Kennealy knew that the man would help him. "What's the job," Triplett said. "What do you want me to do?"

Kennealy told him, and Triplett listened intently for the few minutes it took. When Kennealy finished Triplett remained silent for a few moments before he finally spoke. "I won't carry a gun," he said.

"That's up to you, Abel."

A few more moments passed, and then Triplett said, "All right, I'll do it. Which one do I get?"

"Shoe."

"I've heard the name."

"Does he know you?" Kennealy asked.

"He might," Triplett said, "but not by sight. Where do I find him?"

"I think we'll find both of them at the St. Charles tonight," Kennealy said. "Can you, uh, afford to close down for a while?"

"You saw the line outside." Triplett said.

* * *

They dressed to leave O'Grady's room.

"What are you going to do?" Lisa asked.

"I'm going to walk around for a while," he said. "Somebody else must know what LeClerc knew. I want to see if I can find that someone."

It wasn't a total lie. He was going to talk to LeClerc's partner that very night, but as far as she was concerned he was simply looking for the man. Instead of lying, he was just leaving her several steps behind him.

"There may be someone I can talk to, also," Lisa said.

"You mean I'm not your only partner?"

She looked at him and said, "I mean I might have another contact. Why don't we both see what we can find out and then get together again tonight."

"For dinner," he said.

"All right."

"A late dinner," O'Grady said. "Say, nine o'clock?"

"Why so late?"

"I have a feeling the police might be talking to me again today," O'Grady said.

"They probably think that if they bother you every day you'll confess."

"I don't have anything to confess."

"They'll never believe that, will they?"

"I hope they will," he said, "or I might never get out of New Orleans."

"Once we have the gold," she said, "they won't be able to stop us from leaving."

They stepped out into the hall, and she kissed him quickly. "I'm going to my room first. I'll see you later tonight."

He nodded and watched her walk down the hall to her own room. He'd never been in her room. For all he knew she had someone in there with her, another partner. Maybe somebody else she thought she was playing for a sucker. Maybe the man who killed both LeClerc and the policeman. Then again, maybe she didn't have another partner at all. There was no point in dwelling on it. He'd find out the truth sooner or later.

He decided to go and find a saloon. There wasn't much he could do before he met with Shoe later that evening, and he didn't want Lisa to see him around the hotel until nine.

Once in her room Lisa Carlson undressed. Naked, she stood in front of her window and stared down at the street. She didn't care that someone might see her standing in the window naked. She had never met a man like Canyon O'Grady. Most of the men she had known over the years were only after one thing. She'd never known a man before who was concerned with her pleasure as well as his own. It bothered her that Canyon O'Grady might end up dead after this.

She knew that if she let Clapton have his way he'd kill O'Grady now. Clapton saw O'Grady as more of a danger than a help. Lisa was actually starting to think that Clapton might be right. Only she was thinking that O'Grady might be a definite danger to Clapton, because if she had O'Grady, why would she need Clapton.

Of course before she got rid of Clapton, she had to make sure that she truly did have O'Grady. The one thing she knew about Clapton was that, although the man was a killer, she could control him. At the moment she could not say the same about O'Grady. In fact, when she was in Canyon O'Grady's arms, when she was in his bed, she was afraid that he could probably get her to do anything *he* wanted. And for that reason alone maybe she should let Clapton kill him.

She had never before known a man she couldn't simply use and discard without a second thought. Canyon O'Grady delighted her, and he frightened her. She had to decide whether or not she was willing to let a man go on doing that.

18

Street.

Following Shoe's instructions O'Grady used a back
stairway so that he could leave his room and the hotel
without going through the lobby. He found himself in
a hallway behind the kitchen, which took him to a door
that led outside. He found Shoe waiting there for him.
It was dark out, and darker still back there because
there were no lights. He took a moment for his eyes
to adjust to the darkness and then noticed that nearby
was a pile of refuse from the hotel. Shoe saw him
looking at it and nodded.

"Yeah," he said, "that's where they found the dead
policeman."

"Nobody's life should end up in a pile of garbage,"
O'Grady said.

"I agree," Shoe said, "but there's not much I can
do about it now. Come on. Let's get moving. If we're
late our pigeon is gonna fly."

O'Grady followed Shoe along behind the hotel and
then down some side streets. It was obvious that the
little man was trying to lose anyone who might be
following them. O'Grady hadn't noticed anyone but
figured Shoe was just playing it safe.

Finally, when they had to be half a mile or so from

the hotel, Shoe stopped and hailed a passing horse-drawn cab. "Basin Street," he told the driver after he and O'Grady had climbed into the back of the cab.

"Where on Basin Street?" the man asked.

"Anywhere," Shoe said. "Just take us to Basin Street."

The man shrugged and shook his horse's reins to get the cab moving.

Shoe turned to look behind them.

"Anything?" O'Grady asked.

"No," the little man said, "but that don't mean that somebody ain't there."

"Kennealy doesn't strike me as the kind of man who would be easy to lose," O'Grady said.

"I ain't worried about Kennealy," Shoe said. "Kennealy ain't gonna kill nobody. Besides, Kennealy ain't been following me. He's knows I'd spot him. If anything, he's got somebody else on me, somebody I don't know."

"Somebody you managed to lose, I hope?"

"If I ain't," Shoe said, still looking behind them, "then he's a ghost, 'cause I can't see him."

"Did Kennealy talk to you as you expected?" O'Grady asked.

"A real short talk," Shoe said. "It was too short. No, if I know Kennealy, he's got somethin' planned, but at least we don't have to worry about him tryin' to kill us. Right now I just don't want whoever killed LeClerc and the policeman to be followin' us."

Now it was O'Grady's turn to look behind them, but he couldn't see anything either.

"Don't worry," Shoe said. "Even if somebody is followin' us, we'll lose him on Basin Street."

When they reached Basin Street O'Grady saw what Shoe meant about losing anyone who might be following. The street was teeming with activity, people filling the streets. They were walking, dancing, and hawking. The air was filled with music, and the whores were out in full force. No matter which way he looked every vice known to man was available. He had been in some rough cowtowns, boomtowns, some of the most wide open towns in the West, and he had never seen anything like this.

"Amazin', ain't it?" Shoe asked.

"Unbelievable is more like it."

"Well, come on. We got some walkin' to do. If anyone can follow us through this and stay with us, then he deserves to."

O'Grady had to agree because *he* had enough trouble keeping up with Shoe on Basin Street. At almost every storefront he passed somebody was pawing him, offering him sex—"the most beautiful girls on Basin Street, friend"—gambling—"the most honest games in the city"—or drink—"the best whiskey this side of the Mississippi." If it wasn't a male hawker trying to draw him inside, it was an underdressed, overly madeup prostitute trying to press up against him and entice him into a room, an alley, or even a doorway for "the best girl flesh you ever had."

People were constantly getting between him and Shoe, who was rushing headlong in front of him without ever looking back to make sure that O'Grady was still there. It fell entirely to O'Grady to make damn sure that he stayed with the little man.

On two occasions they entered an establishment which O'Grady assumed was where they were going to have their meeting, only to continue on right through to the back door, outside again, and back to Basin Street.

Just when O'Grady was starting to wonder when the people and the vice opportunities would end, Shoe stopped abruptly, putting his hand out to stop O'Grady in his tracks.

"We're goin' in here," Shoe said. "It's a whorehouse. Our man is going to be upstairs. I'll have to go up and talk to him first. You stay down here and try to keep your hands off the girls."

"I'll do my best," O'Grady said. "Whores are not exactly my idea of a good way to spend money."

"These are," Shoe said. "This is the highest quality whorehouse in N'Orleans. The best girls, and best *lookin'* girls, and the cleanest."

"If you say so."

"You'll see," Shoe said. "Just remember when we get inside. Don't go upstairs until I come back down to get you—and pick out a girl. It's got to look like we're goin' upstairs to do business. Understand?"

"I understand."

"All right, let's go."

Shoe took one more look both ways and behind them, and then pushed the doors open to enter the whorehouse with O'Grady close behind him.

At first O'Grady experienced relief. There was music, but it was subdued, and there was no crowd around him, poking and prodding and trying to sell something.

"Little Shoe," a woman said, approaching them,

"*mon cher*, how are you?" The woman appeared to be a well-preserved fifty or so, although she was undoubtedly tightly corseted. Her breasts swelled out from her low-cut gown as if they were about to burst. She bestowed a kiss on Shoe, seeming to have a genuine affection for the little man.

"Is he here, Josephine?" Shoe asked.

"*Oui*," she said, "just as you said. He came in and went upstairs with Vivienne."

"This is Canyon O'Grady," Shoe said, introducing the big agent.

The woman looked at him with admiring eyes and said, "*Magnifique*. He is quite beautiful, no. My girls will fight over him."

"He's not here for your girls, Josephine," Shoe said. "Just let him pick out one to go upstairs with, but not until I come back down. Understand?"

"*Oui*, little one," she said. "I understand."

"And don't call me that," Shoe said, scolding her. She did not act as if he had scolded her however. She simply smiled at him with such affection that O'Grady became convinced the corseted woman was in love with the small man.

"Go with her and wait," Shoe said to O'Grady.

They entered a living room filled with scantily clad women. Some men were in the room also, but so few that there were sometimes two and three women to a man, and still some women sitting together or on their own.

Shoe moved forward and chose a petite Chinese girl with small, pointed breasts and very long, black hair. He took her by the hand and led her to a stairway up to the second floor.

"Look around," Josephine said to O'Grady, "see what you like."

That was going to be a problem. O'Grady was not there to choose a woman, which was just as well because he didn't see anything he *didn't* like.

19

O'Grady moved into the living room among all the women, first giving up his hat to a black man wearing a tuxedo. The men in the room looked at him, and then let their eyes slide away. The women looked at him, and their eyes stayed on him; they devoured him. Canyon O'Grady was a man who made women think. After he was gone an hour they would still be thinking about him. Even the prostitutes, the professionals who made men pant for a living and pay for the privilege, wondered about him. What would he be like?

He looked around and, just to pass the time, tried to decide which woman he would want if he were there for that purpose.

They appeared in all shapes, sizes, and colors. The woman Shoe had taken upstairs had been the only oriental, but there were two black girls, countless blondes and brunettes, and two redheads. There were tall, slender girls with no breasts and wonderful butts; there were tall, slender girls with big, round breasts and slim hips and butts; there were girls who had it all—breasts, hips, and butts—but who weren't pretty; and there were girls with faces like angels, but with very slender, flat bodies. One girl looked fifteen but was probably a nineteen-year-old who was supposed to look fifteen. There were small, slender women and small, full-bodied women, women in their twenties and women in their thirties, a few in their forties, even a handsome-looking woman with gray hair and a body most thirty-year-olds would kill for.

He was finally able to pick one out—an adorable little blonde with an angular jaw, wide, blue eyes, small breasts and hips, but beautiful, creamy skin. She was wearing something filmy and blue, something you could almost see through. When he got near he could smell her, clean and fresh, probably from a bath. Shoe had said they were clean women. Maybe that meant they bathed after every customer.

"Hello," he said.

She looked up from the sofa where she was sitting alone and said, "Hi."

"What's your name?"

"Kathleen," she said. "Would you like to sit?"

"Sure," he said, seating himself on the sofa next to her.

"Did you come in with Shoe?" she asked.

"That's right."

She nodded.

"Why?"

"We were told that a man would come in with Shoe and that he would pick one of us, but that when we went upstairs with him we wouldn't have to do anything."

"Does that sound unusual to you?" he asked.

She smiled. "I've been doing this for a long time, mister,' she said. "Nothing is unusual to me."

"A long time, huh?"

"That's right."

"How long?"

She gave him a long, level stare and said, "Long."

"What are you," he asked, "twenty-five, twenty-six, maybe twenty-eight?"

She laughed now, a lovely sound that made him smile.

"I'm thirty-nine," she said.

He didn't believe her. "What?"

"You heard me," she said. "Don't make me say it again, okay?"

O'Grady looked across the room at the girl who looked fifteen. "She looks fifteen, but I'm guessing twenty."

"She's twenty-five," Kathleen said.

"I must be slipping," he said. "I used to be good at guessing people's ages."

"Don't feel bad," she said. "In this house we create illusion; that's what we're here for."

"What about you?" he asked. "Do you ever dress up as fifteen?"

"No," she said. "I could you know. I'm small enough to do it, but I don't like to."

"Why not?"

"The men who pick you are generally mean," she said. "They want to tie you up and spank you, or they want you to tie them up and spank them. You're not like that."

"Are you asking?" he said.

"No," she said, "I'm saying you're not like that. I can tell by looking at you."

"All that experience, huh?"

"That's right."

They sat quietly for a while, very little space between them. He became convinced that the heat he was feeling was coming from her.

"So?" she asked.

"So . . . what?"

"Am I the one?"

"Which one?"

She grinned at him. "The one who's going to go upstairs with you tonight?" she asked.

"Oh," he said, "you mean to do nothing?"

"That's up to you, isn't it?" she asked with a shrug that was as adorable as the rest of her. "You might decide to stay awhile."

She was refreshing, this whore. Honest, straightforward, no pretensions—not at the moment, anyway. She was more honest than Lisa Carlson, that much was for certain. "Maybe," he said to her, "maybe."

She ran her index finger up and down his arm, then poked him and said, "I hope you brought enough money."

"Oh," he said, frowning, "I never pay for it, Kathleen. It's not a habit I've gotten into."

"Really?" she asked, looking at him with interest. "You know, most of these men, they wouldn't be here if we were giving it out for free. They're here because they want to pay for it. It's funny, the way men are."

"I feel the same way," he said, and then after a moment added, "about women."

She laughed at that, a hearty, genuine laugh.

Josephine came walking over and looked down at them with her arms crossed. "Is this the one?" she asked him. "Kathleen?"

He looked up at her, and then at Kathleen, who was smiling. "Yes," he said, "Kathleen."

"All right, then," Josephine said. "Take him to your room, Kathleen dear, and make sure the gentleman enjoys himself."

Kathleen stood up and put her hand out to O'Grady, at the same time looking at Josephine with an amused look on her face. "I don't know," she said, "he might not be the only one who enjoys himself."

Kathleen hauled O'Grady to his feet with surprising strength and led him by the hand to the stairway Shoe and the oriental girl had gone up earlier. She released his hand as they started up the stairs, and he walked along behind her, admiring her taut little behind. She was so small, probably no more than four foot eleven, and yet he was sure she was like a stick of dynamite, small but powerful, maybe even dangerous.

Upstairs she took his hand again down the hallway to her room. She opened the door and led him inside, closing it behind them.

"Now what?" she asked, leaning her back against the door.

"Now we wait, I guess," he said.

"For what?"

"For Shoe."

She walked slowly to the bed and sat down. It didn't make a sound beneath her weight. She slid off one of her slippers, crossing her leg on her knee and started rubbing her small foot. "What are we supposed to do while we wait?" she asked.

O'Grady stared down at her. He knew what he would have liked to do while he waited, but he was working now, and he couldn't afford to give in to those desires. "Jesus . . ." he said, and she smiled.

"That might be the nicest thing anybody ever said about me."

"Jesus . . ." he said again, shaking his head.

* * *

131

They talked a little while, and she actually settled down on the bed and relaxed. He ended up liking her a lot, enjoying the time they were spending while waiting for Shoe—although he still would rather have been in the sheets with her, touching her, tasting her, holding her . . . Shoe, where the hell are you?

Just then there was a knock at the door. He held his hand out to stay her and moved to the door himself. "Who is it?" he asked.

"Shoe," a voice said. "Open the damned door."

O'Grady opened the door just enough for Shoe to slide in. When the little man saw Kathleen sitting on the bed he looked up at O'Grady with a sly look. "Good choice," he said.

"Shoe," O'Grady said, "when are we going to do what we came here to do?"

"Now," Shoe said. "Just up the hall. Let's go." He opened the door and slid out again. O'Grady paused and looked back at Kathleen.

"Hurry back, lover," she said, waggling her fingers.

"Not tonight," he said, regretfully.

"Well," she said as he was closing the door, "don't forget me."

Little chance of that, he thought, as the door snapped shut.

O'Grady followed Shoe up the hall about three doors.

"You go in," Shoe said. "I'll wait out here."

O'Grady thought for a moment, then said, "What the hell, Shoe. You can come in. We're partners, right?"

"Right," Shoe said, "but he don't want me in there. He wants to talk to you." He stepped back from the door and bowed from the waist in an "after you" motion.

O'Grady knocked on the door, then opened it slowly and went inside. He was in the room before he realized that Shoe hadn't given him the man's name.

20

The man lounged on the bed, much the way Kathleen had been in her room, only he wasn't doing it with as much style. Nor was he really as relaxed as he wanted to seem. He was a gray, dirty man in his early fifties with thin wisps of hair that didn't seem to want to lie down on his head. They just floated around him.

"You the one?" the man asked.

"Which one?" O'Grady asked.

"The one who was with Anton."

"LeClerc?"

"Yeah, LeClerc," the man said, "what are we talkin' about here?"

"I didn't even know Anton LeClerc."

The man sat up straight and stared at O'Grady. "Then what are we doin' here?" he demanded.

"Look," O'Grady said, "what's your name?"

"Whataya wanna know my name for, huh?" the man asked, suspiciously.

"I have to call you something," O'Grady said.

"Call me . . . I don't know, call me . . . call me Amos."

O'Grady had a feeling that Amos was the man's real name. He just wasn't able to come up with something else at the moment. "All right, Amos," O'Grady said, "just sit quiet and let me explain something to you."

"Did you kill Anton?"

"No," O'Grady said, "I didn't kill Anton."

"Then how come—"

"Just shut up and listen, Amos," O'Grady said. "I got Anton LeClerc's name from a friend of mine in Washington. LeClerc was going to lead me to something, something big, and he was going to get a piece of it, a big piece."

"Who in Washington?"

"That doesn't matter," O'Grady said, "what matters is that LeClerc got killed before he could tell me what I needed to know."

"And you didn't kill him?"

"I told you I didn't kill him, Amos," O'Grady said impatiently. "Haven't you been listening?"

"Yeah, yeah," Amos said, "I been listenin'."

"All right," O'Grady said. "Now, if there was someone else who could give me what LeClerc was going to give me, I'd be willing to come across with a big piece."

Amos blinked a couple of times, then leaned forward. "Tell me somethin'," Amos said.

"What?"

"If Anton knew where it was—whatever it was— why would he need you, and why would he need you to give him a piece? Why wouldn't he give you a piece?"

"Because without me," O'Grady said, "LeClerc wouldn't get anywhere near it. He wouldn't have the nerve. He could know where it was, and he wouldn't be able to get anywhere near it. That's why he'd need me, or somebody like me."

Amos stared at O'Grady, then sat back on the bed again, his back against the bedpost.

"Are you like that, Amos?" O'Grady asked. "Is that what you're like?"

Amos looked at O'Grady for a moment, then his eyes slid away and started looking around the room.

"You know what we're talking about here, don't you, Amos?" O'Grady asked.

Amos didn't answer.

"Amos!" O'Grady said. "Come on. Do you know what Anton knew? Can you help me? Because if you can, you'll be helping yourself, too."

Amos hunched his shoulders. He looked as if he wanted to crawl up inside himself and hide.

"If you wait for someone else, Amos," O'Grady said, "you're going to end up with someone who will slit your throat when he's got what he wants."

"And how do I know you won't slit my throat?" Amos asked.

"Because that's not the way I do things, Amos," O'Grady said. "You've got to believe me, or neither of us is going to come out of this with anything."

Amos remained silent, thinking. The process seemed painful to him.

"Amos," O'Grady said softly, "you know what we're talking about here, don't you?"

He waited, watching the man on the bed, and when Amos spoke he said one single word, in a whisper. "Gold."

O'Grady smiled and said, "All right . . ."

As it turned out Amos didn't exactly know where the gold was. "I know everybody Anton knew though," he said, "and I know everythin' Anton knew. If I don't know where it is, and I can't find somebody who knows where it is, I can figure out where it is."

"How can you do that?" O'Grady asked.

Amos smiled for the first time since O'Grady had entered the room and said, "All I have to do is think like Anton."

O'Grady wondered just how much effort that would really take.

O'Grady stepped out of the room and found Shoe waiting in the hall. The little man might have had his ear to the door, but somehow O'Grady doubted it.

"So?" Shoe said. "What have we got?"

"A beginning," O'Grady said. "We've got a beginning."

"He don't know nothin'?"

"He knows something," O'Grady said, "He just doesn't know what he knows, yet. He just needs a little time."

"To do what?"

"To think like Anton LeClerc."

Shoe frowned in disbelief and said, "I know bar rags that can do that!"

"Everybody can't be as smart as you, Shoe."

"Don't I know it."

"Come on," O'Grady said, "let's go."

"What's your hurry?"

"What?"

"You got somethin' else to do?" Shoe asked. "Someplace else to go?"

O'Grady opened his mouth to answer, then stopped when he realized that the answer was no. There was nothing to do now but wait for Amos to come up with something, as long as Amos didn't end up dead.

"Maybe we should stick with Amos, Shoe," O'Grady said.

"That won't work, Canyon," Shoe said. "Where he's got to go he's got to go alone. Too many people around, and he won't find out anything. Why don't we just stay here awhile?"

"Here?" O'Grady said.

"Sure," Shoe said. "What's the hurry. If we were followed here, and somebody's waitin' outside, let 'em wait."

O'Grady thought about Kathleen, who was probably still in her room.

"Canyon?"

O'Grady looked at him.

"We can stay for free," Shoe said. "You won't have to pay a penny."

"Why?"

"Josephine likes me," Shoe said. "Come on, one night of relaxation won't hurt you."

O'Grady knew he could go back to the hotel right now and get into bed with Lisa Carlson, but it wasn't Lisa he was thinking about at the moment.

"I'll be in here," Shoe said, indicating the door opposite the room Amos was in. "Just knock when you want to leave."

Shoe waited a moment for O'Grady to protest, and when the big redhaired man didn't, he grinned, opened the door, and went inside.

O'Grady turned, walked down the hall to Kathleen's room, knocked, and entered. She was sitting right where he had left her, but she was naked. Her small, pink-tipped breasts were perfect, and the entire room smelled of her.

"I knew you'd be back," she said.

He smiled, closing the door behind him, and said, "It must be all that experience. . . ."

21

Abel Triplett hated Basin Street. In his old age Triplett hated anything that put him into direct contact with other people. In that regard, Basin Street was the worst place in the world for him.

He had followed the man called Shoe every step of the way, in spite of the little man's attempts to be sure that he and O'Grady were not followed. Although Triplett had not worked in many years, the old ways came rushing back to him. All through his life Abel Triplett had virtually been able to do whatever he set his mind to—except live with what he had become. In his forties he had looked back at his life of tracking, hunting, and killing for money, and had not liked what he saw. So he decided to settle in New Orleans. Unfortunately Jerry Kennealy had also settled there, and Triplett owed Kennealy his life. He had been waiting a long time for the policeman to collect, and now he was wondering if this was it. After all, Kennealy had told him not to feel obligated at this time, that he was not invoking the old debt. Why then, Abel Triplett wondered, was he standing across the street from Basin Street's finest whorehouse late at night, waiting for Shoe and O'Grady to come out.

* * *

Jerry Kennealy was having much the same thoughts. He was standing behind Josephine's whorehouse, still stinging from having allowed Canyon O'Grady to get out of the St. Charles Hotel without seeing him. If Triplett hadn't sent a messenger to get him and bring him to Basin Street, Kennealy might still be at the St. Charles waiting for O'Grady to make a move.

This turn of events only served to convince him that he had done the right thing recruiting Abel Triplett. The man had always been the most amazing tracker Kennealy had ever known, and he had been able to turn that talent to following someone like Shoe, who knew New Orleans well and was very adept at not being followed.

So O'Grady and Shoe were in the whorehouse, and Kennealy was sure they were not there for the same reason as other men. Obviously they were meeting someone, but for what purpose? As far as Kennealy or Inspector Quitman could see, there were still no motives in the killings of the two men, Anton LeClerc and the unfortunate policeman. Perhaps tonight was the night they'd find out what was going on.

Ben Clapton loved Basin Street. He loved the activity going on around him, loved the pulse of the street and the excitement and fear that hung in the air. Most of the people were there out of desperation, and he fed on that.

Clapton had followed Jerry Kennealy from the St. Charles to this location after telling Lisa Carlson that Canyon O'Grady had managed to slip out of the hotel.

"I want to know where he went, Ben," she said. "We're supposed to be partners."

"We're supposed to be partners, Lisa," Clapton told

141

her. "Forget about O'Grady. He has no intentions of sharing anything with you."

"And you do?"

"Yes," Clapton said, "I do."

They were in her room, and she had put her hand on his face. At that moment he had the urge to tear off her clothes and throw her down on the bed. The truth of the matter was he still had not been to bed with Lisa Carlson, and it was because of that he did not give in to his urge. When they finally did go to bed together he wanted to savor the moment.

"How can we find out where he went?" she asked, stroking his face.

"The policeman," he said. "He's still downstairs in the lobby. He'll get word somehow."

"Then follow him," Lisa said. "Then send a messenger to get me."

"And what about O'Grady?"

"If he's betrayed me," she said, "you can kill him tonight."

Clapton had smiled at that and said, "Yes . . ."

Now he had sent the messenger to the St. Charles and was waiting for Lisa Carlson to arrive. When she discovered where her precious O'Grady was Clapton knew he'd finally get his chance to put Canyon O'Grady to rest.

Lisa Carlson waited in her room impatiently for a messenger from Ben Clapton. As good as Canyon O'Grady made her feel, if he had betrayed her then he had to die. She would not allow another man to use her and betray her without making him pay for it. She only hoped that they would be able to find the gold before she had Clapton kill him.

The man called Amos was in fact Amos LeClerc. No one knew that Anton was his brother. Amos remained alone in the room and wracked his brain. His brother, Anton, had been bragging for the past couple of weeks that he knew something—something about hidden gold—that was going to mean a lot of money. Amos, of course, had been afraid that his older brother was going to get himself killed, talking to the wrong people, and that apparently had happened. But Anton was dead, and there was nothing Amos could do about that now. All he could do was fend for himself. If he could figure out what Amos knew about the gold, maybe he could figure out where it was. Once he did that he knew he would not have the courage to get it himself any more than his brother did. He was going to have to depend on Canyon O'Grady.

Amos believed O'Grady when he said he had not killed Anton. For some reason he felt that the man was telling the truth. He didn't know who the man was, or how he had come to be here looking for the gold. He would probably never know that, but somehow he felt he had to trust him. All he had to do now was give O'Grady something he could work with.

Inspector George Quitman stared nervously at the man sitting across from him. Many years had passed since Quitman last saw the man, until a few weeks ago when the man had arrived in New Orleans.

"It's time for the South to make its stand, George," the man had told him.

"What do you want me to do?" Quitman had asked.

The man told him about the gold. Apparently the loyal southerners who had hidden it were now dead.

All that was known was that the gold was in New Orleans. They did not know where.

"Where do we look then?" Quitman asked.

"We don't," the man said. "We let others do the looking. When they find it, that's when *we* move."

"I haven't the men I can trust—"

"The men will be brought in, and placed under your command. Once you have recovered the gold, you will be commissioned into the Confederate Army as a major. Your first mission will be to deliver that gold."

"And will you be here?"

The man shook his head. "I must go back to Virginia to get everything ready," he had said. "This mission is yours, George. I trust you with it."

"Yes, sir," Quitman had said, "you can depend on me."

Quitman had been waiting for weeks, and now it appeared that the time was almost near. Anton LeClerc's death, the appearance of the mysterious Canyon O'Grady, the death of the policeman—it all added up. Factions in New Orleans were looking for the gold and would be fighting among themselves to keep it. All Quitman had to do was sit back, watch, wait, and be ready to swoop in and take the gold from whoever won.

In the end the South would be the only winner.

Shoe liked small, oriental women, and he liked them young. That was why he always chose Li when he came to Josephine's. He knew that Josephine loved him, but could never bring himself to bed the Madam herself. She was too old, though several years younger than himself, and too big for him. Li was perfect, and now that she knew what he liked the time he spent with her was relaxing as well as enjoyable.

When he and Canyon O'Grady finally found the goods, and he collected his share, there'd be much more time spent like this, he thought. He was reclining on the bed, his hands behind his head, looking down at Li's head, which was bobbing between his legs. He could feel her tongue on him, and then her mouth came down on him, capturing him inside.

Shoe wasn't a greedy man, and he had stayed alive this long by taking only the cut he had coming to him. He was satisfied that Canyon O'Grady was a man of his word. He didn't know who O'Grady was, or whom he was working for, but all he wanted was his fair cut . . . and to stay alive to spend it.

22

O'Grady's assessment of Kathleen proved to be correct. This adorable little woman turned out to be a bundle of sexual energy that exploded all over him.

After he entered the room she moved to the foot of the bed, on her knees, and impatiently undressed him. "You know all the girls downstairs noticed you as soon as you came in, don't you?" she told him, removing his shirt.

"Did they?"

She leaned forward and ran her tongue over his chest, flicking at his nipples, then went to work on his belt. "Oh yes," she said. "We don't usually get men like you in here, men who don't want to pay for it, I mean. We get some attractive men and some who are good in bed, but they all have that . . . that thing about *wanting* to pay for sex, and then they have a preconceived notion about what sex-for-pay will be."

"Which means?" He lifted his feet, allowing her to remove his boots and his trousers.

"Which means," she said, kneeling on the floor to removed his underwear, "that they don't enjoy it. Oh, my," she said when his rigid penis came into view. She smiled up at him and closed one small hand around him. "You're going to enjoy this, aren't you?"

"No question about it," he said.

She took him into her mouth and he closed his eyes . . .

Later he lifted her up easily in his arms and deposited her on the bed. He got on the bed with her, intending to explore her, but she rolled him over with surprising strength and straddled him. She ran her hands over his chest, then leaned over to kiss him, her full mouth warm and firm. Her tongue blossomed in his mouth, and she moaned as he sucked on it.

She lifted her hips and quite suddenly was impaled on him. He had pierced her easily, for she was wet and more than ready. She was also very hot, not only inside, but her flesh, as well. He reached for her small breasts, covering them with his hands as she proceeded to ride up and down on him. He thumbed her nipples, and she bit her bottom lip and let her head fall back. Her shoulder-length blond hair hung down behind her. Her belly moved, and he found his eyes drawn to her navel. It seemed a ludicrous thought, but he decided that she had the most beautiful navel he had ever seen. He touched it with the tip of his index finger, then slid his finger down and, while she rode him, he touched her swollen clit. She gasped then, and a series of tremors ran through her body, causing her to increase her tempo. She was bouncing up and down on him, coming down heavily each time, as heavily as she could since she probably weighed no more than ninety-five pounds.

He reached up to cup her face, then slid his hands down to her shoulders, her breasts, and down again

147

over her ribs until he was holding her by the waist and then the hips.

Suddenly he grasped her hips and lifted her off him.

"No . . ." she protested, but he paid no attention. He turned her over so that she was lying on her back, and then he started exploring her, finally, with his mouth.

He kissed and licked her nipples, sucking them into his mouth and flicking them with his tongue. They were incredibly hard like pebbles. He kissed and licked his way down her body, pausing at her beautiful navel to probe it with his tongue, and then continued on down until he was tasting her, her wetness on his cheeks and chin. She moaned and lifted her hips, holding his head with both hands and rubbing her crotch against his face with each probe of his tongue. She murmured, "Oh, yesss," as another series of tremors wracked her body. He held her fast, not allowing his mouth to lose contact with her until she began to plead with him to get back inside her.

Finally he relinquished the hold his mouth had on her, moved up, and entered her. Her short but powerful legs came up and encircled him. He slid his hands beneath her to cup her buttocks and pulled her to him with each thrust.

"Oh, God . . ." she moaned, "Jesus . . . Canyon . . . my God, I'm on fire."

It could have been whore talk, but he didn't think so. She sounded more sincere in her pleasure than Lisa Carlson, although he was equally sure that neither of them had to fake their pleasure. Kathleen probably appreciated it more because she was used to faking it for her clientele. In point of fact, *real* pleasure was something that Kathleen wasn't used to, and experiencing it now was a revelation to her.

She reached for his buttocks, but her arms were too short, so she settled for groping at his back and then raking it with her nails as, once again, a fire started from deep inside her and blossomed outward until it ignited an explosion. . . .

Behind the whorehouse Jerry Kennealy thought he must be getting old. There was a time when he never would have risked lighting a cigar at a time like this, but he felt such a need for the smoke that he decided to take the chance. He cupped the match, trying to hide its flame, lit the cigar, then extinguished the match. He also cupped the cigar in his hand so that when he drew on it his palm hid the glowing ember.

The damage had been done however.

Amos LeClerc sat up on the bed in amazement. He couldn't believe it, but he seemed to have come up with the answer to the riddle without even having to leave his room. Replaying much of what Anton had been saying for the better part of a month, Amos felt sure he knew where the gold was.

O'Grady got up from the bed and moved to the window. He felt a certain degree of guilt at having taken the time with Kathleen, but he quickly dispelled the thought. She was an amazing woman, and he was glad he had not passed up the experience.

He looked out the window, which overlooked the back of the house. For a moment he couldn't believe what he saw on the ground, but there it was—the flare of a match and in its light the unmistakable face of Jerry Kennealy.

"What is it?" Kathleen asked from the bed.

"I have to go," he said, grabbing his clothes.

"Already?"

"I can't help it."

She sat up in bed, the sheet falling away from those perfect little breasts, each a comfortable mouthful.

"Will you come back?"

He paused with one leg in and one leg out of his pants, looked at her, and said, "I hope so, Kathleen."

"I hope so, too . . ." she whispered as he finished dressing.

O'Grady hurriedly left Kathleen's room and went down to the door of the room Shoe had entered. He knocked, gently but insistently.

Rather than call out to see who it was, Shoe walked to the door and opened it. O'Grady saw his wizened face peering out from the slit in the doorway. "We've got trouble."

"Like what?"

"Like Kennealy," O'Grady said. "He's out back."

"Shit," Shoe said. "I'll be right there," he added and shut the door.

O'Grady thought that if Kennealy was in the back, somebody had to be out front. Was Kennealy there as a policeman? Or were they in danger of more than just being arrested?

He looked at the door to the room where he had talked to Amos and wondered if the man was still inside. He decided to find out and knocked.

"Who is it?" Amos's voice asked timidly.

"O'Grady."

Amos opened the door and looked up at him. He

150

was only a few inches taller than Shoe, who was stepping out of the other room at the same time. "You're still here," Amos said.

"Yes," O'Grady said, "but we have to leave now."

"I know."

O'Grady frowned. It didn't sound like the man was reacting to what he had said.

"You know what?"

"I know where the gold is."

Shoe moved next to O'Grady and said, "Are you sure, Amos?"

"Pretty sure."

"How could you be?" O'Grady asked. "You never left that room."

"It was stuff Anton said," Amos replied.

"Amos," O'Grady said, convinced that this was the man's real name after all, "what was your relationship to Anton LeClerc."

Amos hesitated, then said, "He was my brother."

O'Grady and Shoe exchanged a glance. "Can you take us there?" Shoe asked.

Amos hesitated before answering, then seemed to make a decision. "Yes."

"Okay, but we have to get out of here first," O'Grady said.

"What's wrong?" Amos asked.

"The police are outside," Shoe replied.

"How?" Amos asked, immediately frightened. "How did they find us?"

Shoe looked uncomfortably up at O'Grady and said, "We must have been followed."

O'Grady looked down at the smaller man and could see how painful the admission was to him. "Forget it," O'Grady said. "Let's just figure out a way to get out of here."

"We don't have to figure it out," Shoe said. "Let's just go and talk to Josephine."

23

"There is an escape hatch," Josephine said.

"A hatch?" O'Grady asked.

"It leads to an underground tunnel," she said. "A lot of the old buildings here have them."

"Can we use it?" O'Grady asked.

She looked at the three men, then asked Shoe, "Will I have trouble with these policemen?"

"I don't think so," he said.

"They'll probably just ask you questions," O'Grady said. "Answer them honestly, Josephine, and you should have no difficulty."

"Very well," she said. "I'll show you the hatch."

She led them through her kitchen into a back store-room. "You must move those barrels," she said, pointing. There were quite a few of them, but working together O'Grady, Shoe, and Amos LeClerc managed to clear them away fairly quickly.

"There," she said, "that is the door."

It was a wooden door with a hole that O'Grady was able to fit two fingers into. He pulled up, and the door opened, revealing a dark hole beneath it.

"Here's a lamp," Shoe said, taking one from the wall. As they lit it he asked O'Grady, "How did you know Kennealy was outside?"

"I saw him," O'Grady said. "He was lighting a cigar, and I saw his face in the light of the match."

"He must be getting old," Shoe said, then he stopped and said, "unless he *wanted* you to see him."

O'Grady looked at Shoe and said, "Let's not start getting jumpy. There was no way he could know that one of us would be looking out the window at that moment. Besides, why would he want us to know he was there?"

"To make us react," Shoe said, "like we are now, sneaking out."

"How would he know where this tunnel leads?" O'Grady asked.

"I don't know how he knows anything," Shoe answered. "He just does."

"Never mind," O'Grady said. "Let's just use this tunnel and do what we have to do."

O'Grady took the lamp and held it to the mouth of the tunnel. There was a wooden ladder going down, and he went first, followed by Shoe, and then Amos.

"Good luck," Josephine said to them, or probably to Shoe.

The hatch above them was replaced.

O'Grady held the lamp aloft and saw that the tunnel extended both ways. "Which way?" he asked Shoe.

"I don't know," Shoe said with a shrug. "There's probably an exit either way."

"That way," Amos said, pointing right.

"Why that way?" O'Grady asked.

"Because that's the direction the gold is in."

"Where is it?" Shoe asked.

Amos looked at Shoe and then at O'Grady and shook his head. "I won't tell you," he said, "I'll take you."

"That's fine," O'Grady said. "You lead the way and we'll follow."

Kennealy was leaning against a fence, looking up at the back of the building. There were still lights on inside and probably would be for some time. Whores worked late, after all.

He took a last drag on his cigar and then tossed it to the ground. As he went to step on it he noticed something odd. There seemed to be a light *beneath* the house. He saw it only because the foundation of the house revealed some spaces. Was it somebody in a root cellar? The light seemed to be moving, as if someone was carrying a lamp. It was probably just someone getting something out of a storage area, but Kennealy knew that this part of town had a myriad of tunnels beneath the surface, tunnels that could be used as escape hatches.

The light was gone now, but he started walking in the direction he had seen the light moving. If he was standing above a tunnel how far could it extend before it came to an exit?

He had gotten burned once tonight. O'Grady had probably gone out of the St. Charles through a back exit, and maybe now he was doing the same thing, leaving the whorehouse by some sort of an escape route.

He began to move faster. If he was wrong, he'd know soon. If he found no exit hatch, he'd simply return to the rear of the whorehouse. For now he moved along behind the Basin Street buildings at a trot, looking for something that resembled a door or a hatch of some kind.

* * *

Beneath the surface they passed other wooden ladders leading down to the tunnel, which undoubtedly led up to other buildings. "This tunnel is shared by a lot of buildings," O'Grady said. "A lot of people probably know about them."

"Including the police?" Shoe said.

"Probably."

O'Grady felt drafts from several different directions and realized that there were some gaps in the tunnel ceiling, probably leading to the outside, and that their light might be visible outside if someone happened to be looking in the right direction. Wasn't that how he had spotted Kennealy—looking in the right place at the right time?

Abruptly, Kennealy changed direction. He decided to take the offensive. He ran back in the other direction, around to the front of the building on Basin Street and across to where Abel Triplett waited.

"What's wrong?" Triplett asked.

"We're going inside."

"Why?"

Kennealy explained about the possible escape tunnel.

"Then you go inside and check it out," Triplett said. "I know where most of these tunnels come out. If they were going in the direction you say, I might be able to spot them."

"All right," Kennealy said, "but let's move now."

Lisa Carlson arrived just as Kennealy came running across the street.

"Look!" Clapton said.

"What?"

"That's the policeman."

"What's he doing?"

"Shh."

They watched, and then Kennealy and Triplett split up, Triplett coming down the street toward them.

"Move back," Clapton said, pressing Lisa into the shadows of the doorway. After Triplett went by they stepped out again. "What's going on?" she asked.

"O'Grady was in that whorehouse, but I'm getting the feeling that's not the case anymore."

"What do we do?"

"We follow that fellow," Clapton said, pointing to Triplett, "and hope that he's too busy to notice us. Come on."

They came to a three-way fork, tunnels branching off in three directions. "Now what?" O'Grady asked.

"Think about it," Shoe said. "That one has to lead to the river. We don't want to go there."

"This one," Amos said, pointing to the right fork.

"Why that one?" O'Grady asked.

"It's this way," Amos said.

O'Grady looked at Shoe, who said, "Hey, we are following *him.*"

"All right, Amos," O'Grady said, "lead the way."

As instructed by O'Grady, Josephine told Kennealy the truth. Of course O'Grady hadn't told her that she had to show Kennealy where the tunnel hatch was, but she carried the truth as far as it would go.

Armed with a lamp of his own, Kennealy dropped down into the tunnel. The dirt of the tunnel floor was loose enough to hold tracks, and he started to follow.

* * *

Triplett knew that the tunnels extended beneath the ground like river tributaries. He ignored the direction of the river and also discounted Basin Street. If O'Grady and his party were smart, they'd want to come out away from Basin Street.

Triplett turned right and moved away from the river as well as Basin Street. Had he not been so out of practice, he would have noticed that the follower was now being followed.

24

"Anton said he was around when the gold was being hidden," Amos said.

"How did he manage that?" O'Grady asked.

"He was always around when things were happening," Amos said. "Nobody ever paid any attention to him—to us."

"Did he know it was gold?" Shoe asked.

"No," Amos said, "in the beginning he just thought it was something valuable. Later he discovered what it really was. By then the building was up, and it was too late to do anything."

"And you're sure it's in that building?" O'Grady asked, looking across the street.

"I remembered what Anton said about that building," Amos said. "That it was a lot more valuable than people thought. And he was always making remarks like that whenever we passed it. Once he said the building was as good as gold, but I didn't know what he meant back then."

"And now we do," Shoe said. He looked at O'Grady and said, "It's kind of ironic, isn't it? That the gold should be hidden there?"

O'Grady nodded and looked across the street again

at the building. He'd been inside that building a couple of times already. He shook his head, not believing the gold was hidden within the walls of the building that housed police headquarters.

Triplett knew that he was on O'Grady and the others through pure luck. He had chosen the correct direction and had seen them coming out from the ground. He then followed them to where they were now, across the street from the police building.

He didn't have any idea what was going on.

"Who is with O'Grady?" Lisa Carlson asked.

"I don't know," Clapton said. "They must be his real partners."

"And what are they doing across the street from the police department?" she asked.

Clapton, studying the building, said, "It was built within the past ten years."

Lisa looked at him quickly, as if they were both thinking the same thing. "The gold is in there?" she asked.

"They must have hidden it in the walls or the floor when they built it," Clapton said.

"If that's true," she said, "what do we do now?"

"Now," he said, "we have to get rid of O'Grady."

"What about his partners?"

"Look at them," Clapton said. "They're street rats. With him dead, they won't have the guts to do anything."

"And what are we going to do?" she asked. "Look where the gold is."

"As long as we know where it is," he said, "we can get to it."

"How?"

"Let's deal with that later," he said. "Right now we have to deal with O'Grady."

"With a policeman looking on?" she asked. "Across from the police department?"

"Well then," he said, "we'll just have to deal with the policeman first."

Once Kennealy came out from the tunnel he knew he had lost O'Grady and the others. There was no way to track them through the streets. He had two choices. He could go back to the hotel and hope to pick them up there, or he could go to the police station to discuss the situation with Inspector Quitman.

He made up his mind.

No matter how good your skills once were, when you've been inactive for as long as Abel Triplett, they start to deteriorate. Of course Ben Clapton's skills were far from eroded. The end result found Abel Triplett lying on the ground, unconscious.

"Don't kill him," Lisa said. "We don't need another dead policeman."

Triplett wasn't a policeman, but the belief that he was saved his life.

O'Grady, Shoe, and Amos remained across the street from the police building. O'Grady was trying to figure his next course of action and finally decided there was none. That the gold was in that building actually turned out to be perfect. All he had to do was pass the information on to Rufus Wheeler, who would then send in some of his uniformed men to collect it.

"So," Shoe asked, "what do we do now?"

"Nothing," O'Grady said.

"What do you mean, nothing?" Shoe asked. "You backin' off?"

"No, I'm not backing off," O'Grady said. "I have some people who can take care of this."

"More partners?" Shoe asked.

"No, not partners," O'Grady said, "but they will be safer than us trying to go in there and get it ourselves."

"Wait a minute . . ." Shoe said.

"Do we still get our cut?" Amos asked.

"Everybody gets paid, Amos," O'Grady said.

Amos looked at Shoe and said, "Then I don't care. As long as I get paid."

Shoe rubbed his jaw. Getting paid without having to go into the building was starting to sound good to him, too. He was just wondering who these people were that O'Grady suddenly had access to. He was getting a real uncomfortable feeling about his partner.

"Hands in the air, boys," a voice said from behind them.

Shod hunched his shoulders. Talk about uncomfortable feelings.

"I'm disappointed in you, Canyon," Lisa Carlson said to O'Grady.

"Lisa," O'Grady said. There was no surprise in his voice. "Don't tell me you didn't trust me."

"Not for a moment, darling," she said.

"Forget that," Clapton said.

162

"Who's this?" O'Grady asked. "Your other partner?"

"I'm her only partner, friend," Clapton said. "You're about to find that out the hard way."

"Am I?" O'Grady asked.

He started to turn and Clapton said, "I didn't tell you to turn around."

"Then shoot me," O'Grady said, completing his turn, "but remember where we are. If you fire your gun, the street's liable to be filled with policemen in seconds."

"New Orleans police?" Clapton said, laughing. "You got the wrong idea about the law in this city, friend."

"Maybe I do, and maybe I don't," O'Grady said. "Maybe there're just enough men inside that building willing to do their jobs to make it uncomfortable for you if you fire that gun."

O'Grady watched the man turning the threat over in his mind. He felt Shoe fidgeting by his side and hoped that the little man wouldn't get brave. He knew he didn't have to worry about Amos.

He waited for Clapton to make his decision.

Kennealy came upon the tableau and pulled up short. They made quite a small crowd, five people standing across the street from the police building. He recognized O'Grady right away and the woman from the hotel. Then he saw Shoe standing next to O'Grady. The other two men were strangers to him, but he could see one thing for sure. One of the other men had a gun and was pointing it at O'Grady.

Kennealy looked around for Triplett but didn't see him anywhere. He drew his gun and started to work his way across the street, hoping he wouldn't be seen until it was too late.

"Come on," O'Grady said, "make up your mind. Pull the trigger or I'll have to take that gun away from you and feed it to you."

He felt Shoe tense next to him.

A smile spread across Clapton's face. "Do you think you can do that?" he asked O'Grady.

"Try me."

"You know," Clapton said, "I think I'll do that. I like it better using my hands anyway."

O'Grady remembered the dead policeman, remembered that Quitman had said that the man had been strangled by someone strong.

"Here," Clapton said, handing the gun to Lisa. "If the other two move, shoot them."

"Ben," she said, "wait, don't . . ."

"This won't take long," he assured her, flexing the fingers on both hands.

He looked at O'Grady and told him, "Come on, big man."

O'Grady was thinking fast. He could fight with the man and get killed. He could fight with him, beat him, and be shot by Lisa. Or, he could do something totally unexpected. He made up his mind.

He drew his gun and shot Ben Clapton dead.

Amos LeClerc screamed.

Shoe jumped and ducked.

"Jesus—" Lisa said. She started to turn her gun on O'Grady, but a voice from behind her stopped her.

"Don't do it!" Jerry Kennealy said.

She froze.

Kennealy stepped forward and relieved her of her

gun. She stared down at the dead Clapton, a look of shock on her face.

Kennealy bent over the man to check him, found him to be quite dead. He then turned and looked at O'Grady. "You've got a lot of explaining to do."

25

Once again O'Grady sat in a room inside the police station. With him were both Inspector Quitman and Jerry Kennealy. Shoe and Amos were being held in another room, as was Lisa Carlson. Kennealy had found Triplett unconscious and had sent him home. He had assured the man that the debt was paid. Triplett walked away muttering something about knowing when you're getting old. Kennealy wondered if he was talking about himself or about him.

"You expect me to believe that?" Quitman asked O'Grady.

"Ask the woman," O'Grady said.

"I've already spoken to her," Quitman said. "She won't say anything."

"Of course not, she's in shock. What about the other two? Shoe and Amos?"

"Those two river rats?" Quitman said. "You'd lie and they'd swear to it. Start telling a better story, O'Grady."

"Look," O'Grady said, "I've told you all along I'm just passing through. I met Lisa Carlson, and we liked each other. Clapton was her boyfriend. He found out about it and decided to do something about it."

"So what happened outside this evening had nothing to do with the deaths of Anton LeClerc or my man?''

"That's right.''

"What were those other two doing with you?''

"They were my guides.''

Quitman looked at Kennealy, who didn't say anything.

"I could throw your ass in jail, O'Grady.''

"For what?''

"For killing Clapton.''

"That was self-defense.''

"For killing LeClerc then.''

"You can't prove that,'' O'Grady said. "A good lawyer would have me out in no time. It would be a waste of your time.''

Quitman stared at O'Grady, then looked at Kennealy. "Jerry, why don't you see to the release of the others?''

Kennealy hesitated, then nodded and left the room. As soon as the door closed Quitman took out his gun and held it to O'Grady's head.

"Where's the gold?''

O'Grady had to admit he was surprised. "What gold?''

"Don't play games with me, O'Grady,'' Quitman said. "Everything that's been going on has to do with the gold. You were looking for it, and LeClerc was going to help you. Clapton and the girl were probably looking for it, too. You recruited Shoe and Amos to help you.''

"And you?'' O'Grady asked. "You're looking for it?''

"That gold can do a lot of people a lot of good,'' Quitman said.

O'Grady looked up at Quitman for a few seconds, then said, "In the South, you mean?"

"That's right," the other man said, "in the South."

"Think about this, Quitman," O'Grady said. "That gold can get a lot people killed. It can start a war that will tear this country in two."

"This country is already torn in two," Quitman said. "We're going to bridge the gap and join it under one leadership."

"Jeff Davis?" O'Grady asked.

"It doesn't matter who," Quitman said. "It's not the man, it's the ideal."

"Jesus," O'Grady said. All along the one thing he hadn't wanted to confront was a zealot, and now he was face-to-face with one.

"How long have you been here, Quitman?" he asked, "in New Orleans?"

"I was sent here years ago, in anticipation of this time," Quitman said, "a time when that gold would have to be found."

"And you were going to let others find it for you, then take it away from them."

"Why not?" Quitman asked. "The superior intellect, O'Grady. Let others do the dirty work for you."

"That's the kind of thinking you want running this nation, huh?"

"Never mind," Quitman said. "Just tell me where the gold is."

"I don't know, Quitman."

"Of course you do."

"If I did, what would I have been doing playing around outside with the woman and her boyfriend? Hanging around with Shoe and Amos? Wasting time in a whorehouse?"

"You were in the whorehouse looking for the gold," Quitman said.

"In a whorehouse?" O'Grady asked. "I'm telling you for the last time, Quitman—"

Quitman pressed the barrel of the gun harder against O'Grady's head and said, "You've got five seconds."

"How are you going to explain this, Quitman?" O'Grady asked. "Shooting an unarmed man in the head?"

"The men in this building are loyal to me."

"The men in this building aren't loyal to anything. No wonder you don't have a viable police force. You're like the others, just marking time—except Kennealy. How are you going to explain it to him?"

"He'll believe whatever I tell him," Quitman said. "He trusts me."

"He won't," O'Grady said, "not after he finds you in here with a dead, unarmed man."

"I'll say you jumped me."

"And you pressed the barrel of the gun to my head and shot me, singeing my hair?"

Quitman thought about that outcome and seemed to see the logic of it.

"All right," he said, backing away. "From here, then."

At that moment Kennealy came back into the room. He saw Quitman holding a gun on O'Grady and frowned. "What's going on?" he asked.

"Nothing," Quitman said, holstering the gun.

"We were having a talk, Kennealy," O'Grady said, "about the department. I'm afraid I said something to upset the inspector."

Quitman glared at O'Grady, then pointed a finger at him and said, "This isn't over." He turned to Kennealy. "Get him out of here. Don't let him leave the city." Quitman stormed from the room, leaving the door open.

"And the others?" O'Grady asked.

"They've already been let go."

"The woman, too?"

"You won't press charges," Kennealy said, "so she's free to go, too. Come on, get out."

O'Grady hesitated. He had to send a telegraph message to Wheeler, telling him where he thought the gold was hidden. After that all he'd have to do is stay alive until Wheeler's men arrived.

Would Quitman try to have him killed? And what about Lisa? Would she hold a grudge or chalk it all up to experience? Or try to find a new partner to go after the gold? Or even try to recruit him again?

And of course he had to hope that after Wheeler's men finished searching the building they actually did find the gold. Given everything that Amos had recalled Anton LeClerc saying, it seemed like a pretty safe bet.

26

On the morning of the second day Rufus Wheeler's men arrived. He must have had them set to go as soon as he heard the word. O'Grady was at the police station when they got there, pulling up in front in half a dozen buggies, twenty men who then proceeded to practically take the building apart. O'Grady did not participate but he watched with interest in the company of Jerry Kennealy.

When Quitman arrived he immediately sought out Kennealy and asked, "What's going on?"

"I don't know," Kennealy said. "These men are from the government, and they had the proper papers that say they have the right to . . . to do what they're doing." Holes in the walls and floors were visible from where O'Grady, Kennealy, and Quitman were standing.

"Are they just tearing the place down or . . . or looking for something?"

O'Grady could tell from the look on Quitman's face that he had answered his own question.

He was not around when the men finally turned up a chest filled with solid gold bars.

Before leaving New Orleans O'Grady took care of a few things. He arranged with Kennealy for the police not to stop Lisa when she left the city by train. He also arranged with Wheeler, via telegraph message—to have Shoe and Anton LeClerc paid a generous reward for aiding in finding the gold.

As for Inspector Quitman, he never did return to the police department, and before he left O'Grady heard from Kennealy.

"It's funny," Kennealy said.

"What is?" O'Grady asked.

They were at the station, waiting for O'Grady's train to leave for Washington.

"I was thinking about leaving the police department and New Orleans altogether."

"And now?"

"Now I'm being promoted, so I'll have a little more to say about how things are run."

"Is that worth staying around for?" O'Grady asked.

Kennealy thought it over a moment and then said, "It's worth staying around to see if I can say a little more about how things are run. If not . . . well, I can still leave."

"I wish you luck," O'Grady said.

"I have the feeling," Kennealy replied, shaking O'Grady's hand, "that this wish is coming from a man who has a lot of his own luck."